"I'm not who I used to be, and people in this town are never going to get past that."

"Well then, they're just ignorant. Don't they realize you're too damned old to be prancing down a runway in a tiara?"

Meri laughed. "Gee, thanks."

"It's true. You're too old to be a beauty queen and too beautiful to be bothered by the pettiness of someone who should know better than to run their mouth."

She cocked a grin at him. "Are you complimenting me, Jack Barlow?"

"Hell, no. Gentlemen compliment women, and I am no gentleman."

He closed the gap between them and touched her cheek, and her heart tripped. She was sixteen again, thinking there was no one in the world she'd ever love as much as she loved Jack Barlow. Then he'd broken her heart, and she'd vowed to never, ever let anyone get that close.

When he brushed her hair back behind her ear and told her she was beautiful, she forgot her promise to herself. She'd thought about him kissing her—did she want him to kiss her? How would it be, after so many years? Better? Sweeter?

THE BARLOW BROTHERS: Nothing tames a Southern man faster...than true love!

Dear Reader,

I'm ridiculously excited to be writing for Special Edition and to be starting a whole new series with the hunky Barlow Brothers! I love connected books—love reading them, love writing them—and especially love writing about family dynamics in large, loving families. In *The Homecoming Queen Gets Her Man*, I introduce Jack Barlow, the former military man with a secret to keep from his old girlfriend, former beauty queen Meri. I had so much fun bringing in his brother Luke and the Barlow family. Like all families, they are far from perfect, which is what makes them so fun to write about!

I have a large family myself—three brothers and a sister. It was never quiet in my house, and even now, when we all get together as adults, we still have some of the same jokes and teasing as when we were kids. My dad is also former military (as is my husband) so I always feel a special affinity for military heroes.

This time, my hero suffers from PTSD, something I knew very little about. I called on Colonel (Retired) Keith Landry, PhD, who served in Iraq and Afghanistan and knew a lot about the subject. He and his lovely wife, Nia, have been fans for a while—and even highlighted one of my older book titles in their wedding last year. So a huge thank you to him for reading passages and giving me feedback on those critical sections.

I hope you enjoy the first Barlow Brothers book!

Shirley

The Homecoming Queen Gets Her Man

Shirley Jump

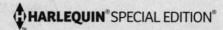
HARLEQUIN® SPECIAL EDITION®

Recycling programs
for this product may
not exist in your area.

ISBN-13: 978-0-373-65861-9

The Homecoming Queen Gets Her Man

Copyright © 2015 by Shirley Kawa-Jump, LLC

Printed in U.S.A.

New York Times and *USA TODAY* bestselling author **Shirley Jump** spends her days writing romance so she can avoid the towering stack of dirty dishes, eat copious amounts of chocolate and reward herself with trips to the mall. Visit her website at www.ShirleyJump.com for author news and a booklist, and follow her at Facebook.com/shirleyjump.author for giveaways and deep discussions about important things like chocolate and shoes.

Books by Shirley Jump

Harlequin Romance

Visit the Author Profile page at Harlequin.com for more titles.

To all the brave heroes in our military,
but especially to my husband and my father,
who have demonstrated true heroism many times,
both in the military and in life.

Chapter One

Five years ago, Meri Prescott left Stone Gap, North Carolina, with a fire in her belly and a promise that *if* she ever came back, she'd be doing it in style. She'd imagined riding down Main Street in the back of a limo while the blue-haired ladies at Sadie's Clip 'n' Curl gawked and the fishermen who parked their butts and their one-that-got-away stories on the bench in front of the Comeback Bar shook their heads and muttered about the good old days when a two-tone Chevy was fancy enough for getting around town.

Meri had imagined a homecoming that would tell everyone in this nowhere town that she had made it, become more than anyone imagined. That she was more than just a pretty face, someone who worried about her manicure but not her grade point average. A girl, really, who had thought New York City would be the cure for all that ailed her, and that in that giant city she had finally found the person she was meant to be, not one who had been manufactured like a store mannequin.

Okay, so she'd been blinded by the stars in her eyes. The Meri Prescott who had left Stone Gap with a tiara and a plan was not the Meri Prescott who was returning. Not by a long shot. And she wasn't so sure Stone Gap was ready to accept the woman she had become.

Frankly, she didn't give a damn either way. She was here for Grandpa Ray, for as long as he needed her. To help him, and in the process...help herself.

Her fingers drifted to her cheek, to the long, curved scar that had yet to fade, a constant memory of the division between her past and her present. There were nights when she woke up in a cold sweat, reliving the attack outside her crappy outer-borough apartment. She'd tried, tried so hard to stay in New York, to keep up with her photography job, but the city had changed for her, and the buildings she used to love had become like prison walls.

She needed air and space and warm sun on her face. Then maybe she'd be able to conquer the demons that haunted her nights and shadowed her days. Maybe then she'd be able to hold a camera again and see something through the lens besides the face of her attacker.

Maybe.

At the stop sign holding court in the intersection of Main Street and Honeysuckle Lane, her ten-year-old Toyota let out a smoky cough. The car's AC had stopped working somewhere back in Baltimore, and exhaust curled in through the open windows, a sickly sweet stench that made it seem like she hadn't journeyed very far from the congested streets of Brooklyn.

All it took to remind her that she was back in the small-town South was a glance out the window, at the wide verandas fronting the pastel Colonials lining Main Street, yielding after Honeysuckle Lane to quaint storefronts with happy flags and bright awnings, sporting first names as though they were residents, too. Joe's Barber Shop. Ernie's Hardware & Sundries. Betty's Bakery. And then one that made her slow, almost stop.

Gator's Garage.

One glimpse of the blue building, fronted by a hand-painted sign fashioned out of an old tractor-trailer tire, and Meri was fifteen again and getting her first clumsy kiss from Jack Barlow—and a year later, going through her first clumsy breakup. She remembered the smell of the motor oil, the dark spreading stain of it in the center of the garage floor, and most of all, Jack's blue eyes, sad and serious, as he told her they were over. That he wanted more than a beauty-queen girlfriend, he wanted someone grounded, real. The words had stung and stayed with her long after he'd shipped out for the Middle East a week later. She'd headed in the opposite direction, to the Miss Teen America beauty pageant, and vowed to forget Jack Barlow ever existed.

A horn honked. Meri jerked her attention back to the road, and a moment later, Gator's Garage was behind her. She took a right on Maple, a left on Elm, then turned again on Cherrystone and faced the house she had left in her rearview mirror five years ago.

It sat at the end of the cul-de-sac like a presiding queen, two stories of white clapboard with porches that stretched from end to end on both stories. The driveway flared out in pale bricks, laid before the Civil War and still flanked by twin willows draped with Spanish moss. It could have been 1840 instead of the twenty-first century, and in some areas of life inside that house, the world still ran as if Abraham Lincoln reigned in the White House.

The Toyota coughed again, jerked like an asthmatic, then sputtered to a stop in front of the house. *Great.*

Meri let out a long breath, but it did little to ease the tension in her neck, the tight band between her shoulders. With the car engine quiet and dead now, the North Carolina heat began to bake her in place.

The urge to turn around, to flee, to avoid what was coming, surged through her. Instead, she pulled out the keys and clasped them in her hand. The hard metal indented her palm with a dose of reality. She wasn't running back to New York, not today, maybe not for a long while.

She had good reason to be here, one frail eighty-four-year-old reason. Grandpa Ray trumped everything else going on in her life.

Meri's mother came out onto the front porch and crossed her arms over her chest. Meri could have spotted the look of disapproval and disappointment on Anna Lee Prescott's face from the space station. She knew that look, knew it far too well.

Still, the masochistic hope that things might have changed rose in her chest and burned for a brief second. No, given the look on her mother's face, there was little chance Anna Lee had done a one-eighty in the last five years. The best Meri could hope for was a forty-five-degree turn in the direction of common sense.

Meri ran a quick comb through her wind-blown hair, then headed up the sloping driveway and down the brick path leading to the front porch. Beside her, the manicured lawn unfurled like a lush green carpet, flanked by precisely pruned rosebushes and strategically placed annuals. A wooden swing hung from a long thick oak tree branch, drifting slightly in the breeze. It could have all been a spread in a magazine—and had been, twice, in *Southern Living* and *Architectural Digest*.

Her three-inch heel caught in the space between the pavers and Meri cursed her footwear choice. For hundreds of miles, she'd told herself she no longer cared what her mother thought.

Yeah, right. If that was so, then why had she exchanged her flip-flops for designer heels that pinched her toes and made her calves ache? Why had she spent twenty minutes smoothing the frizz out of her hair in the bathroom at a roadside truck stop?

Did I really think wearing heels and straightening my hair would make this easier?

Yeah, she had. Way to go, lying to herself.

When Meri reached the first porch step, an automatic smile curved across her face, as if she were stepping onto a stage instead of into her childhood home. All that practice had been good for something, it seemed. She could still prance around in high heels and look happier than a bird in the sky. "Hi, Momma."

"Why, as I live and breathe," Anna Lee said, emerging from the door frame to grasp Meri's hand with both of her own. "My prodigal daughter has returned."

Meri leaned in and pressed a kiss to her mother's cheek. She caught the faint scent of floral perfume, mingled with the oversweet fragrance of hair spray and the mild notes of the powder dusting her flawless makeup. Everything about Anna Lee was as manicured and perfect as the lawn. Tawny hair sprayed into a submissive bob, white cotton shirt and navy shorts pressed into straight lines, and subdued, pristine makeup.

Anna Lee drew back and cupped Meri's cheeks in her soft palms. "You look so worn-out, honey. Are you sleeping well? Eating right?" Her thumb skipped over the scar and she averted her eyes, as if pretending she hadn't seen the red line would make the whole horrible thing disappear. "Why don't you come in, splash some cold water on your face and get a little makeup on? You'll feel right as rain."

Irritation bubbled inside Meri, but she widened her smile and kept her lips together so she wouldn't say something she'd regret. "It was a long drive, Momma. That's all."

Anna Lee's thumb traced a light touch over the scar running down the left side of Meri's face. "Is it…?"

Meri captured her mother's hand and drew it down. "I'm fine, Momma. Really."

Her mother looked as though she wanted to disagree, but instead she nodded and pasted on a mirror smile to Meri's. "Let's get out of this heat. I swear, I'm about ready to melt into a puddle, just stepping onto the veranda."

Anna Lee drew out the syllables in true Southern belle tones, whispers tacked on the end of her consonants. Meri always had liked the way her mother talked, in a sort of hushed song that drew people in, captivated them.

And had captivated two husbands, both deceased now, God bless their souls, leaving Anna Lee a very wealthy woman. She had returned to her Prescott roots, the more respected name of her first husband, as if the second husband had never existed, a mistake she had erased.

Although Jeremy Prescott had come from the other

side of town, he'd shed his past as if shaking mud off his boots and managed to put himself through school and make millions in investment banking before a heart attack took him down at the age of fifty. Meri had never understood why her father hadn't wanted to be like his simple, homespun family—the very people Meri loved the most. Grandpa Ray was one of the most real people Meri had ever known, living in his cabin by the lake, a planet away from the son and daughter-in-law who had made their life in this over-manicured mansion.

Meri let her mother hustle her in and down the polished hall, because it was easier than trying to stop the tidal wave of Anna Lee. They took a left and entered the rarely used formal sitting room, where cushions held their shape and dust motes held their breath.

In five seconds, Meri realized why her mother had led her here. The room glistened with gold and silver, shining on glass shelves mounted against two walls. A rainbow of ribbons hung from a custom-made display rack, while a thousand rhinestones sparkled their way through the rows and rows of crowns.

Meri sat on the stiff white love seat, its curved lion's feet pairing alongside her nude pumps. Her mother perched on the rose-colored armchair across the room, divided from her daughter by an oval mahogany coffee table and an Aubusson carpet that had cost more than a small car. The antique grandfather clock in the corner ticked away the moments with a beat of heavy, unspoken expectations.

Meri shifted in her seat. God, it was like being in a mausoleum. "Momma, wouldn't we be more comfortable on the back porch?"

Her mother waved off that suggestion. "There are *men* out there."

She said the word *men* as if referring to a plague of locusts. Anna Lee never had liked to be around those who performed manual labor. Maybe she was worried they might put a broom or a hammer in her hands.

"They are building a gazebo," Anna Lee went on. "You know me, always changing this, fixing that."

"Making everything perfect, especially your daughter." The words sprang from Meri's lips like a cobra waiting to strike. And she'd tried so hard to be polite and dutiful. That had lasted, oh, five seconds.

Anna Lee's brows furrowed. "All I ever wanted was for you to be all you could be. You were always such a beautiful girl, so capable of—"

"I am not here to talk about might-have-beens, Momma. I'm no longer a beauty queen."

"You will always be a beauty queen. That's something no one can take from you. Why, look at all these crowns." Anna Lee gestured toward the sparkling tiaras, the ribbons, the trophies, all reminders of a different time, a different Meri. "They prove you are the most beautiful girl in all the world."

Meri sighed. "I'm not that person anymore, Momma."

Anna Lee went on, as if she hadn't heard Meri speak. "You could have been Miss America, if you had…" She pursed her lips. "Well, that's neither here nor there."

They'd had this argument a thousand times over the years. Some days Meri felt like she was arguing with herself, for all Anna Lee heard. "Momma, please. Let's not get into that again."

Anna Lee reached a hand toward her daughter's face, toward the pale red scar that arced down Meri's cheek like an angry crescent moon. "If you'd just let me take you to Doc Archer, he could fix you up and make you perfect again."

"Don't start, Momma. Just don't start."

Anna Lee let out a long sigh. "Well, you think about it."

Meri had thought about it almost every day for the past three months, since the attack that had left her with the scar, changed in a thousand ways. But her mother still saw her as the same girl who had won a hundred beauty pageants, the one who had been destined for Miss America before she ran out of town and ditched everything and everyone.

She should have stayed in the car, kept driving, and avoided this senseless argument. When was she going to accept that her mother was never going to change?

Meri got to her feet and summoned up a little more patience. If she could have avoided stopping here, she would have, but after talking to Grandpa Ray a couple days ago, she'd been hell-bent on getting home and seeing him again. Which meant, for now, dealing with her mother. "Can I please get the key to the cottage so I can get settled in?"

Her mother waved behind her. "It's in the same place as always. Though I don't understand why you'd insist on staying in that shack when Geraldine made up the bed in your old room."

Meri didn't answer that. She crossed to the antique rolltop desk, pulled out one of the tiny drawers on the right-hand side and retrieved an old skeleton key. When she was a little girl, her daddy would use the guest cottage on the weekends for fishing—and, Meri suspected, time away from Momma and her endless list of expectations. A few times, Daddy had taken Meri along. She'd reveled in those days—when she could get muddy and messy, with no one around to straighten her hair or fuss over her meal choices.

As soon as Meri curled her palm around the heavy key, she was sixteen again in her mind, on a starlit night at Stone Gap Lake. She'd snuck down to the cottage with Jack, nervous and excited and completely infatuated. She'd been too foolish, too eager to prove she was mature and ready for what Jack wanted. In the end, she'd sat alone on the bank of the lake, confused and heartbroken.

Her cousin Eli had found her and driven her home, and helped her sneak up the rose trellis to her room before her mother found out she was gone.

Eli.

God, how could he be gone? Just being here, it seemed as if her cousin, with his giant personality, was still alive, that she'd see him at Sunday church or hanging out in the drive-through of the Quickie Burger. He was her best friend, one of the few people who could tease her out of a bad mood or a bad day, and more like a brother than a cousin. But in her head she could still hear that heartbreaking call from her aunt last year, telling Meri he was gone. The realization hit her anew with a sharp ache.

Meri drew in a breath, then tucked the key in her pocket and turned back to her mother. All Meri wanted to do was go see her grandfather, the most sane person on her father's side of the family. "Have you seen Grandpa Ray?"

"I have had a number of commitments. Something I'm not sure you remember, Meredith Lee."

The use of her formal name told Meri two things— one, her mother was trying to gain control of the situation, and two, she was gearing up to launch a criticism masquerading as a compliment. "I'm not here to discuss the past or what I'm doing with my present, Momma. I'm here to see Grandpa Ray, and be with him for as long as…" The words caught in her throat.

Too many losses. Meri couldn't take another. Not now.

Her mother pursed her lips, then nodded. She waved a delicate, manicured hand. "Then go, go. But be back in time for supper. Geraldine is making roast chicken. She made up your bed with those floral sheets you like, if you change your mind about where you want to stay."

Meri sighed. "You knew I wasn't staying here. Grandpa needs me, so I'm staying at the cottage. Nobody's living there, and it's right next door."

"Why, Meredith Lee, that is akin to sleeping in the woods. Your grandfather lives like a heathen and that guest cottage of his is no better. Good Lord, when was the last time he cleaned it? It could be positively infested. I don't think anyone has been there since your father used to go for his fishing weekends."

"Just because Grandpa Ray lives in a modest house and doesn't give a rat's a—" she cut off the curse before it fully formed "—care about what people think of the way he lives doesn't make him a heathen."

"Geraldine will be sorely disappointed."

The maid had been with the family for thirty years, longer than Meri had been alive. She had no doubt the gregarious woman would miss having Meri around, and for a moment, Meri felt bad about that. Then she realized her mother had said *Geraldine* would be disappointed, not herself.

Nothing had changed. Nothing at all. "I have to go, Momma."

She hurried out of the emotionally stifling house and into her car. She whispered a prayer, then turned the key and with a jerk the Toyota roared to life. Thank God. As soon as she pulled out of the driveway, the lump in her throat cleared and the air smelled sweeter. She wound her way through town, passing the statuesque old South mansions, the quaint storefronts, the moneyed world of Stone Gap, until she reached the southwestern corner, so disparate from the rest of the town it seemed as forlorn as a stepchild, forgotten and left behind.

This was where Meri fit in, where she could breathe. This hardscrabble section of town, where people let their lawns get overgrown and left bikes in the front yard and didn't care if someone forgot a glass on the coffee table. She parked in Grandpa Ray's stone driveway, kicked off the heels and switched them for the flip-flops she kept stowed under the passenger seat, and got out of the car. She swooped her hair up into a ponytail as she walked, and by the time she reached the porch, Meri felt like herself.

For half a second, Meri expected her cousin Eli to come loping down the street, with his ready smile and another one of his corny jokes. But as she gazed at the empty blacktop, the truth hit her again like a brick. Eli was dead. He had died in the war, on some dusty road in Afghanistan, and he wasn't coming back. Not now, not ever.

But his spirit was still here, in the clapboard houses and the big green trees and the happy birds chirping from their perches. In the trees he had planted years ago, the windows he'd helped Grandpa install, the gazebo he'd spent an entire winter building. Eli would have wanted

Meri to be happy, to enjoy the day, whether it was short or long, and to never let her grief stew.

And she was going to try her best to do just that.

Meri charged up the bowed front steps and banged on the screen door. "Grandpa? It's Meri!"

No response. She called again, but got only silence. Her stomach lurched. Was Grandpa sick? Had he passed out? Or…

She heard a sound from behind the house, and the fear and worry ebbed. She hurried down the steps, skirted the paint-weary house, ducking under the Spanish moss hanging from an oak tree, a genuine, light smile already on her face before she rounded the last corner.

"Grandpa Ray, you silly man," she said with half a laugh, "don't tell me you're already ignoring the doctor's—"

The words died in her throat. Her gaze skipped past her grandfather, napping in the Adirondack chair, and stopped when she saw the only man in Stone Gap she never wanted to see again.

Jack Barlow.

He stood there, a hundred feet from her grandpa, with an ax in one hand and a pile of chopped wood at his feet. He wore an old hunting cap, the camouflage brim tugged down over his short dark hair. His khaki shorts looked as if they'd been through a shredder, and his concert T-shirt was so faded that only the letters *R* and *H* showed, but still—

He looked *good*. She hated that he looked so…grown-up and confident and strong. And sexy. The Jack she remembered had been a gawky teenager just growing into his height. He'd headed out to boot camp, then on to the Middle East, and come back—

With the body of a Greek god.

He arched a brow in her direction and she cut her gaze away. Damn. He'd caught her staring.

Jack put down the ax, wiped the sawdust off his hands, then crossed to her. He'd gotten taller, leaner, more defined, and her traitor stomach did a funny little flip when he closed the gap between them. "Figured it was only a matter of time before trouble showed up," he said.

"Nice to see you, too, Jack."

He grinned, that lopsided smile that had once melted her heart. It didn't have one bit of impact on her now. Not one bit. "Glad to see you haven't changed."

She raised her chin. "I've changed, Jack Barlow. More than you know."

His gaze lit on the scar swooping along her cheek. Her heart clutched and she held her breath. Something haunted his eyes, something darker, edgier, different than anything she had ever seen before. For a second she felt a tether extend between them. Then his gaze jerked away and the connection flitted off with the summer breeze.

"I think we both have, Meri," he said, his voice low.

"Some things will never be the same, will they?" She thought of her cousin, who had gone off to war a little after Jack did, tagging along with his best friend, just as he had when they'd been little and he'd followed Jack to the creek, the lake, whatever adventure the day had in store.

Two had left. One had returned.

Did that thought break Jack's heart as much as her own? They'd been inseparable as kids. Trouble triplets, her grandmother used to say with a smile. Not having Eli here was like missing a limb.

"I've got work to do." Jack picked up the ax and went back to the pile of wood. He swung the metal into the stumps with furious whacks, and kept his back to her, wearing that look of concentration that she knew as well as she knew her own eyes. Message clear: conversation over and done.

One thing was sure—the charming Jack Barlow she had known in high school was gone. There was something about this new Jack, something dark, that she didn't recognize. Was it because of what he'd gone through in the military? Was it the loss of Eli, who had been a best friend to both of them for so many years?

Either way, the turned back and the clipped notes in Jack's voice threw up a big No Trespassing sign, one Meri intended to honor. She was here for her grandfather, not to solve decade-old mysteries. And definitely not to get involved again with the guy who had seen her as nothing more than a vapid, pretty face.

She strode across the lawn and bent down by her grandfather's chair. Meri pressed a kiss to his soft cheek, trying to hide her alarm at how thin, how pale, how frail her once hearty grandfather had gotten. He seemed to be shrinking into himself, this once robust man who used to carry her on his shoulders.

His eyes fluttered open, and then he smiled and grasped her hand with his own. Joy shone in his pale green eyes, gave his wan face a spark of color beneath his short white hair. Behind him, the vast Stone Gap Lake sparkled and danced the sun's reflections off Grandpa Ray's features. "Merry Girl," he said, stroking his palm tenderly against her scar, a momentary touch filled with love. "You're here. How's my favorite granddaughter?"

"Sassy and smart, as always."

He laughed. "You know what tames sassy?"

"Sugar," she replied to the familiar dialogue. Every time he'd seen her, for as long as Meri could remember, Grandpa Ray had asked her the same question and she'd given the same replies. The exchange always ended with the same sweet reward—a handful of miniature chocolate bars.

He gave her a wink and a nod. "I still have a bowl full of candies on the dining room table, waiting just for you." He grinned. "And Jack, if you care to share."

She wasn't sharing anything with Jack Barlow. Not now, not in the future. He was a complication she hadn't expected, but a complication she could surely avoid.

"Me? Share chocolate? Grandpa, you forget who you're talking to." Behind her, she could hear the steady *whoosh-thwap-thud* of Jack's ax splitting wood. Jack was here, helping her grandfather, something he had done for as long as she could remember. Back when they were kids, it had been Jack and Eli, spending their hours after school and weekends helping Grandpa Ray, then dashing into the lake to wash away the sawdust and sweat. For all the heartbreak Jack Barlow had brought to her life, he'd brought something very good to her grandfather's and for that, she was grateful. That little flutter earlier— all due to being surprised at seeing him, nothing more.

Last she'd heard, he was still in the military, fighting overseas. But judging by his appearance here and the buzz cut that was growing out, he was no longer the property of the US government. Not that she cared. At all. Then why did her mind keep reaching back to that moment in Gator's Garage? The painful months after their breakup when she'd tried to forget Jack Barlow and his lopsided grin?

Whoosh-thwap-thud. Whoosh-thwap-thud.

Given the fast and furious pace Jack was attacking the wood, maybe she wasn't the only one trying to pretend that running into each other meant nothing.

Meri blew out a breath and dismissed the thought. Jack Barlow was in her past, the last place Meri wanted to visit. "After this morning, I could use every last chocolate in that bowl, Grandpa."

Grandpa Ray chuckled. "Been visiting your mother?"

"I thought she might have changed. But…" Meri shook her head. She'd done her daughterly duty and gone to Anna Lee's house. That was enough. "Anyway, I'm not here to talk about her. I want to talk about how *you're* doing."

"I'm still warming a seat." He grinned. "That's all I'm asking from the Lord these days."

Her chest tightened, and she felt tears burn the back of her eyes, but she blinked them away and gave Grandpa Ray a smile. She perched on the edge of the opposite chair and took his hands in hers. "I'll be here, as long as you want."

"I'd like that, Merry Girl." His voice wavered a bit and his hand tightened on hers. "I'd like that very much."

She sat back against the chair, turning her face to the North Carolina sun. It warmed her in a way nothing else ever had or ever would. Here, in the backyard of this run-down little bungalow, among the trees and grass and birds, she was home, at peace. Here, she could breathe, for the first time in a long, long time. "Me, too, Grandpa. Me, too."

Then she heard the *whoosh-thwap-thud* again. Her gaze traveled back to Jack, down the muscles rippling along his back and shoulders, and the flutter returned.

Finding peace was going to be a lot harder than she'd expected.

Chapter Two

Forgetting. It wasn't something Jack Barlow did easily.

When he was a kid, his grandmother used to tease him about his incredible memory. Looking back, he didn't think that he had such a great memory as much as a penchant for paying attention to details. That had served him well when he worked in his father's garage and needed to reassemble an engine, and when he'd been on patrol in Afghanistan. In those cases, lives depended upon noticing the smallest things out of place. Still, there were days when he cursed his mind and wished the days would become a blur, the details a blank.

A car door slammed somewhere outside the garage. Jack flinched, oriented his attention in the direction of the sound, adrenaline rushing through his body. To anyone else, it was just a car door, but Jack's brain jogged left instead of right, and in that second, he saw the bright light of the explosion detonating, heard the roaring thunder blasting into the Humvee, then the spray of metal arcing out and away from the impact. Through the floorboards, the passenger seat, up and into—

Eli.

Jack squinted his eyes shut, but it didn't erase the sounds of Eli's agonizing screams, didn't wipe away the sight of his blood on the truck, on Jack, on everything. Didn't make him forget watching Eli's big brown eyes fading from light to glass. Jack shut his eyes, but still all he saw was the moment when he'd turned the truck east instead of west, and the shrapnel intended for Jack hit his best friend instead.

Goddamn.

Jack took in a breath, another, but still his heart jack-hammered in his chest, and his lungs constricted. Sweat plastered his shirt, washing him hot, then cold. The wave began to hit him hard, fast, like a riptide, dragging him under, back to that dark place again.

Blowing out a breath, he unclenched his fists and opened his eyes. He stared up at the underside of the Monte Carlo. The snake lines of the exhaust, the long rectangle of the oil pan. Inhaled the scent of grease, felt the hard, cold concrete beneath his palms. Listened to the sounds of passing traffic. Reality.

Finally, Jack pushed himself out from under the car and into the cool, dim expanse of the garage. He rubbed the tired out of his eyes, worked to uncoil the tension that came from snatching a few minutes of sleep every hour. But still the memories stayed, a panther in the shadows.

Ever since he'd come home from the war, Jack had done the only thing he could—worked until he couldn't stay awake. He divided his days between his father's garage and Ray's cottage, because it was only when he was immersed in a disabled engine or surrounded by a stack of unchopped wood that he could pull his mind away.

Away from the past. Away from the mistakes he had made. Away from his own guilt.

And now, away from Meri. He hadn't expected to see her—not today, not ever—and the encounter had left him a little disconcerted, unnerved. Meri represented everything he wanted to put behind him, everything he wanted to forget—

And couldn't.

How the hell was he supposed to tell her the truth? Tell her that he was the one who should have protected Eli, who should have made damned sure Eli, with his perpetual smile, was the one who came home? How could Jack ever look in Meri's eyes and admit the truth?

That it was Jack's fault Eli had died. Jack's, and no one else's.

He threw the wrench in his hands at the workbench. It pinged off the wooden leg and boomeranged into his shin. Jack let out a long string of curses, but it didn't ease one damned bit of the pain.

"Whew. I'm impressed. I usually only hear language like that when the Yankees lose."

Jack turned, grabbing a rag to wipe off the worst of the grease on his hands, and to give him another second to collect himself, push that panther back into the shadows a little more. His brother Luke stood just inside the garage, looking as though he'd just come from the beach, or a vacation, or both. His brown hair had that lightened tint that came from too much time in the sun, and Jack suspected his brother's khaki shorts had more sand in the pockets than dollars. Unlike their eldest brother, Mac, who worked so much the brothers had nicknamed him Batman because of how rarely he showed up at family events. "You here to help me change out that transmission?"

Luke laughed. "Work? That's against my religion."

Jack leaned against the tool chest and tossed the rag on a nearby bench. "Funny, I don't remember laziness being a lesson in Sunday school."

"That's because you and Mac were too busy trying to compete for teacher's pet." Luke reached into the small fridge by the door, pulled out two sodas and tossed one to Jack.

Jack popped the top and took a long swallow of the icy drink. "And you were too busy trying to ditch."

Luke grinned. "Something I have perfected as an adult."

Jack snorted agreement. He swiped the sweat off his brow with the back of his hand and propped a foot against the front bumper of the '87 Monte Carlo. The car had more miles on it than Methuselah had kids, but long-time customer Willie Maddox refused to junk the Great White Whale. The car was big and loud but classic and sporty, and Willie babied his ride like Evangeline Millstone babied her overdressed, overindulged Chihuahua. Hence the new transmission in the Great White Whale, and a decent payday for the garage. Ever since their dad's knee replacement surgery, Jack had been shouldering the garage—and that meant shouldering the responsibility for his father's income. Another week or so and Bobby Barlow would be back in the garage.

"What do you say you knock off early and we head down to Cooter's for a couple beers?"

"It's three o'clock in the afternoon, Luke."

"All the more reason to celebrate." Luke tipped his soda in Jack's direction. "Come on, you workaholic. The world isn't going to fall apart if you close down the shop a couple hours early. Besides, I hear Meri Prescott is back in town. All the more reason to grab a beer with me."

Jack scowled. "What does Meri being back in town have to do with anything?"

"You telling me you aren't interested?" He arched a brow. "Or horny?"

"Jesus, Luke, let it go." Jack tossed the empty soda into the trash, grabbed the wrench and slid back under the Monte Carlo. He tightened a bolt and waited for the sounds of his brother leaving. Instead, a pair of familiar sneakers appeared in his peripheral vision.

"You still gonna stick to the *I'm not interested in her* line?"

"We dated a million years ago." *Eight*, his mind corrected. "Of course I'm not interested."

Yeah, right. Given the way he'd reacted to seeing her yesterday, and how many times his mind had wandered to thoughts of her, *not interested* was far from the truth. Either way, it didn't matter.

Because getting involved with Meri would mean telling her what had happened to her cousin on that battlefield, and that was one thing Jack couldn't do. Hell, he could barely handle the truth himself. Diving into that deep, dark corner of his mind would pull him down into the abyss, and right now he was barely clinging to the edge.

"Just leave me the hell alone, Luke. I have work to do." There were days when he was glad neither Luke nor Mac had taken to working in the garage. Start talking alternators, and his brothers found other things to do.

It took a while, but eventually Luke's feet moved out of Jack's line of vision, then out of the garage. Quiet descended over the darkened world beneath the Monte Carlo and Jack told himself it brought him peace.

Seems he was just as good at lying as he was at forgetting.

Meri parked in the lot outside of Betty's Bakery, a kissing cousin to George's Deli—a husband-and-wife restaurant venture that had been a staple in downtown Stone Gap for as long as Meri could remember. Every time she saw the bakery and deli, she thought of her cousin Eli, who had worked summers and weekends here with his parents, and who never failed to bring home treats after his shift. Out of all the people Meri had known in the world, Eli had been the most gracious, most giving and most loving. There wasn't a person in Stone Gap who hadn't thought of him as halfway to a saint. When he'd died, it was as if something good and bright had left the world, leaving a sad dimness behind. Here, Meri could still feel Eli's presence. That was nice.

Meri's aunt Betty—her mother's younger and sassier sister—and uncle George Delacorte loved creating food, loved sharing food with their customers, friends and families, but didn't love working side by side, so when their first food venture, a small restaurant they ran together, failed, they moved into two locations as a way to keep the peace in their marriage. Betty provided the baked goods for George's sandwiches, and he kept her stocked with disposable flatware and paper plates. It was, Betty often said, a marriage made in Fleischmann's Yeast.

Aunt Betty and Uncle George had always been jovial people, a trait that Eli had had in abundance. The loss of their only son had dimmed their spirits, but not their giving to the community, Meri saw. Each of the shops sported an American flag, proudly waving in the wind. The front window of the deli held a service star, the blue star changed to a gold one, to represent a fallen soldier.

Meri's heart clenched. She got out of the car and went into Betty's first. The scent of fresh-baked bread and muffins greeted her at the door. Her stomach growled in what her mother would call a most unladylike manner. God, everything smelled so good, so decadent. For a second, the automatic response of *I can't have that* dinged in her head. How many years had she resisted desserts and second helpings and carbohydrates?

"Well, as I live and breathe!" Betty came bustling around the counter, her arms outstretched, her generous hourglass frame outlined with a bright pink apron. "Meri! You are a sight for sore eyes!"

"Oh, Aunt Betty, you, too." Meri returned Betty's boisterous hug, enveloped by the scents of cinnamon and vanilla and homecoming. She had spent many an afternoon at this bakery, watching Betty make everything from doughnuts to rye bread, soaking up the scents of decadent foods along with her aunt's offbeat wisdom. She glanced around the homey space. "I still half expect Eli to walk through the door every time I come here."

"Me, too, sweetheart. Lord, I miss that boy." Aunt Betty shook her head and her eyes welled. Her gaze lingered on a drawing tacked to the wall, a hand sketch of an indigo bunting, a bright blue bird that Eli had always said was a sign of good things to come. For as long as Meri had known him, her cousin had sketched the wildlife in Stone Gap. The two of them had taken many hikes over the years, she with her camera, he with a sketch pad.

Aunt Betty looked at the drawing for a long time, her fingers fluttering over her lips. "He was my heart, don't you know? A mother should never have to bury her son."

Meri nodded, her throat too thick for words. The indigo bunting just stared back from its pencil perch.

Aunt Betty swiped at her eyes and worked a smile to her face. "Well, no more of that. I can just hear Eli now. 'Mama, save your crying for another day. The sun is out, and that's reason enough to smile.'"

"I swear, I never saw him depressed a day in his life."

Aunt Betty's smile wobbled. "He brought everyone who knew him a lot of joy. I'm sure he's got every angel in heaven laughing as we speak."

"I wouldn't doubt it for a second. Probably pranking the Holy Ghost, too."

That made Aunt Betty laugh. "True, so true." She drew back and eyed Meri. "How are you doing, honey pie?"

The concern made tears well in Meri's eyes. Her aunt understood her so well, a thousand times better than Anna Lee ever had. "I'm doing fine. Especially now that I'm back in town."

"To stay?"

Meri shook her head. "To visit. Eventually I'll need to get back to my photography job." Assuming, that was, that she could ever get over her fears to do her job. She'd hoped that coming here, where the world seemed put to rights, would give her back the magic she had lost.

"I saw some of your photographs in a magazine, and Eli used to send them to me over the computer all the time. Such amazing talent you have, Meri." Aunt Betty beamed.

"Eli shared them with you?"

"Of course. He was proud as punch that his cousin was taking the world by storm in the big city. Thought you were the next Ansel Adams. Can't say I disagreed."

Meri reached out and drew her aunt into a tight, warm hug. "Thank you, Aunt Betty. That means a lot, coming from you."

The unspoken message—Anna Lee would have to be on her deathbed to say such a thing. There were many days when Meri wondered how her life would have been different had she been born into Aunt Betty and Uncle George's house instead of Anna Lee's castle on Cherrystone.

As if reading Meri's mind, Aunt Betty shifted the conversation to Anna Lee. "Word has it that you're staying out at Ray's, in the guest cottage. Your mother is positively mortified. She feels like you're, and I quote, 'besmirching the family's good name' by refusing her hospitality."

"I didn't refuse. I made another choice."

Betty cupped Meri's face with her generous palms. Unlike her mother, Betty didn't flinch away from Meri's scar, and in fact, barely seemed to give it notice. "A good choice. Don't let my sister push you around. Lord knows she's been trying to do that since the day you were born. I swear, if she could have, she'd have told the doctor how to arrange the maternity ward and what temperature to warm the formula."

Meri gave Betty another hug, then drew back. "Thanks, Aunt Betty."

"Anytime." Betty swung back behind the counter and readied a white box. "Let me guess. You're here for Ray's daily muffin supply?"

"Yup. Then heading to Uncle George's to pick up

Grandpa's favorite sandwich for dinner. I tried to talk him into some salmon with a side of spinach, but he was having none of that. Said the only thing that makes him feel better is Uncle George's sandwiches for supper and your muffins in the morning."

"Ray's a smart man. But not smart enough to know I make those muffins with whole wheat flour and add some flaxseed to the sandwich bread." Betty loaded a quartet of muffins into the box, closed the lid, then tied it with thin red string. "And what are you getting for you?"

"Oh, I shouldn't." The response came like a Pavlovian reflex.

"Yes, you should. And you can. And don't tell me about calories or fat grams or any of that nonsense. Food is meant to be enjoyed, not ignored. And besides, you deserve it. Why, I bet you already dealt with your mother today."

Meri nodded. "It was as much fun as I expected."

"Then all the more reason to indulge. Talking to Anna Lee will drive you to either sugar or pharmaceuticals. My vote is for sugar." Betty placed a chocolate cupcake covered with fluffy pink frosting in front of Meri. "Cupcakes are like good men. Taste them, savor them and never, ever ignore them or someone else will eat them right up." She nudged the cupcake closer. "So, come on now, quick as a bunny, take a bite."

Meri picked up the dessert, inhaling the rich notes of the chocolate and the sweet confection of the raspberry frosting. She hesitated, then blew out a breath and sank her teeth into the side. Frosting curved on her lip, chocolate cake crumbs dusted her chin, but the bite in her mouth melted like heaven against her palate. She zeroed in for a second bite, then paused when the shop door's bell rang.

And Jack walked into the bakery.

She turned part of the way toward him, the cupcake cradled in one hand, the frosting on her lip. He caught her eye, and something warm and dark extended between them, a whisper of a memory that bloomed in her mind.

Jack, tempting her with a cupcake, the day before a pageant. Telling her the contraband treat would be worth every bite. She'd refused, shaking her head, her body quivering with desire for him, for the chocolate, for everything that she had denied herself for years. Then he'd swiped a dollop of frosting off the top, placed it against her lips, and she'd opened her mouth to taste it, to taste him. Jack's gaze had captured hers, and in that next instant, the cupcake was forgotten, and she was tasting his mouth, his body, him.

He'd been the one to end it that day, pulling away from her, telling her she was right, that she had a pageant to prepare for, and she needed to focus on that. Even then, a week before they'd broken up, he'd been drawing the line in the sand between them.

Aunt Betty greeted him, and Jack said hello back, but his attention stayed on Meri.

"What are you doing here?" she asked.

His gaze flicked to Betty, then away, and a shade dropped over his features. She could see him shutting the door, clear as day. Typical Jack—shut her out to whatever was going on inside his head.

"I'm surprised you're still in town," Jack said, instead of answering her question.

She bristled. "I just got here, Jack. I'm not going anywhere for a while."

"Good."

The single word surprised her, undid the ready fight in her head. "Why do you say that?"

"Because Ray won't admit he needs a mother hen, but he does. And you're the perfect person to tell him what to do."

"Are you saying I'm bossy?"

A half smile curved across his face. "Darlin', you've always been bossy."

Something about the way he said *darlin'* sent heat fissuring through her and made her think of the hot summer nights they'd spent together as teenagers, when temptation was their constant companion.

"I see you still love cupcakes," Jack said, taking another step closer to her.

Heat pooled in her gut. God, how she wanted to just look into his blue eyes and fall all over again. But she already knew where this led, already knew how he truly felt about her.

She put the cupcake on the counter and swept the frosting from her lips with the back of her hand. Who was she kidding? This wasn't a chance to rewrite the past or show Jack she had changed. No, she wasn't here for that. As even Jack had said, her main goal was restoring Grandpa Ray to health. Besides, whatever she might have felt for Jack Barlow when she was a silly teenage girl had evaporated that day in the garage, as fast as rain on hot tar. "I don't think I ever loved them," she said. "I just thought I did."

Chapter Three

Jack pounded out six hard and fast miles on the back roads of Stone Gap. The late-evening heat beat down on him, sweat pouring down his back, but he didn't slow his pace. His punishing daily routine drove the demons back, so he kept on running until his body was spent and his throat was clamoring for water.

What had he been thinking, walking into the bakery yesterday? Did he think this time, finally, he'd get the courage to say what he needed to say? Once a week he stopped in to either Betty's or George's, and every time the words stayed stuck in his throat.

Then, seeing Meri with that little bit of frosting on her lip derailed all his common sense. For a moment, he had been eighteen again, half in love with her and thinking the world was going to go on being perfect and pure. Until he'd gone to war and learned differently.

Damn. Just going into that bakery hurt like hell, and he'd let himself get swept up in a past—a fantasy—that no longer existed. A mistake he wouldn't make again. Add it to the long list of mistakes Jack never intended to make again.

Luke was sitting on the front porch of Jack's cottage in the woods when Jack got back. "You look like you're about ready to keel over."

Jack braced his palms on his knees and drew in a deep breath. Another. A third. "I'll be fine."

Luke scoffed, got to his feet and shoved a water bottle under Jack's nose. "Here, you need this more than me."

Jack thanked his brother, then straightened and chugged the icy beverage. "What are you doing here? Not that I don't appreciate the water, but this makes two days in a row that I've seen you. I didn't see you that much when we lived in the same house."

Luke shrugged. "Mama's worried about you. Mac is off in the big city, pretending we don't exist, working his fingers to the bone, so that leaves me as the designated caretaker."

"In other words, she got desperate."

"I prefer to call it smart."

Jack scoffed. He drained the rest of the water, recapped the bottle, then three-pointed it into the recycle bin. "I gotta go to work."

Luke stepped in front of him and blocked his path. "Promise me you'll be at dinner on Sunday night. Mama said she'd tan us both if you don't come."

"First of all, the last time Mama spanked either of us was when you were six and you stole candy from the general store. You cried, she cried and she never spanked us again. Second of all, I am quite capable of eating on my own. I don't need to show up for the whole family-meal dog and pony show."

"Since when has dinner at Mama's been a dog and pony show?" Luke gave Jack's shoulder a light jab. "And what's up with you, anyway? Don't tell me you like eating those TV dinners on the sofa better than homemade pot roast?"

"Since when did you become my keeper?" Jack shook his head. "I'm busy, Luke. I don't have time for this. I gotta get to the garage."

Luke stood there a moment longer, as if he wanted to disagree but had run out of arguments. A part of Jack wanted Luke to drag him to dinner at Mama's, because maybe being forced to be among the rest of the world would keep that panther at bay. Or maybe it would unleash the damned thing and Jack would ruin the only good he had left in his life.

"Fine, have it your way," Luke said. "Enjoy your Hungry-Man dinners."

His brother left, and Jack headed into the little house on Stone Gap Lake that he'd rented when he came home from the war. It wasn't much as houses went, but it was set in the woods at the end of a desolate street, a mile as the crow flew from Ray's house. If there was one thing Jack didn't want, it was friendly neighbors who'd be popping by with a casserole or an earful of gossip. His mother had wanted him to stay in the family home, but the thought of being around all that…caring suffocated him. He'd rented the first house he found, and told his mother he'd be fine.

He heard the crunch of tires on the road and readied a sarcastic retort for Luke as he headed back onto the porch, where the word died in his throat. Meri sat behind the wheel of a dusty Toyota, sunglasses covering the green eyes he knew so well, her hair tied back in a ponytail. She pulled into the drive, rolled down the window, but didn't turn off the car.

"I need your help. Grandpa Ray is fixing to climb a ladder and clean out the gutters, and refuses to wait for you to help him. He wouldn't let me so much as touch the ladder, and I'm afraid he's going to hurt himself."

Jack let out a curse. "I told him I'd do that tonight, after I got done at the garage."

"You know him. When he wants something done, he wants it done now." She tucked the sunglasses on top of her head. Worry etched her face, shimmered in her eyes. "Can you help? I mean, if you're busy or something—"

"I'm not busy." *Not busy enough*, he should have said. Never busy enough. But Ray needed him, and if there was one man Jack would help without question, it was Ray. And with Meri looking at him like that, as though she'd pinned all her hopes on his shoulders…a part of him wanted to tell her to find someone else. Instead he said, "Give me five minutes to get cleaned up."

"Sure." She put the car in Park. "Thanks, Jack."

He started toward the house, then the nagging chivalry his mother had instilled in him halted Jack's steps. He turned back to Meri. "Uh, you want to come in? Have some iced tea or something? You shouldn't wait in the car in heat like this."

She hesitated a moment. Probably weighing the environment-damaging effects of running the car in Park for a few minutes versus the risks of being around him. "Sweet tea?"

He grinned. "Is there another kind?"

She got out of the car, one long leg at a time. She was

wearing cutoff denim shorts and flip-flops, topped with a V-necked blue T-shirt. On Meri, the casual attire seemed sexier than the elegant dresses she'd worn in her pageants. It seemed more…Meri, if that made sense. More real. Prettier.

Damn.

All these years, and he still wanted her now as much as he had then. Back then, he'd been young and stupid and rash. He'd believed anything was possible in those days. That the world could be set to rights with a lot of laughter and a sweet kiss from her lips.

He knew better now. He knew about dark days and bad decisions and regrets that ran so deep they had scarred his soul. And so he looked away from Meri's legs and Meri's smile and headed into the house.

"Kitchen's over there," he said, pointing down the hall. "I'll be done in a couple minutes."

It wasn't until he was standing beneath the bracing cold water of his shower, the droplets pelting his face, his neck, his shoulders, that Jack could breathe. He pressed his hands against the wall and dropped his head, letting the water rush over his skin until all he could feel was cold.

He stepped out of the shower, dried off and tugged open a dresser drawer. Almost empty. Maybe it was about time he got his crap together and did some laundry. He reached for a ratty T, then stopped when his hand brushed over a worn khaki cotton T, stuffed at the bottom of the pile after his last tour, forgotten until now.

Memories clawed at him. Reminded him exactly why he had rented a house in the woods by the lake, far from the rest of the world. Far from people like Meri.

People who would ask questions like *why*. Questions he couldn't even answer for himself.

Jack cursed, grabbed the nearest plain shirt and slammed the drawer shut again. He finished getting dressed, then headed out of his bedroom. He'd help Ray and stay the hell away from Meri. The last thing he wanted was to have a conversation with her, one where she'd ask about Eli.

The only other person who knew about that day was Jack's commanding officer, who had taken his report, then mercifully left him alone in his grief. Jack had served out the last month of his tour on autopilot, a shell of himself, then come home and done what the psychologist told him to do—tried to put it all behind him and move on.

Move on? Where the hell to?

Meri was standing in the kitchen, her back to him, looking out the back door. Her lean frame was silhouetted by the morning sun streaming in through the windows. His heart stuttered, but he kept moving forward, ignoring the urge to touch her, to get close to her. "You ready?"

She turned and a smile curved across her face. "There's a deer in your yard," she whispered with a sense of awe and magic in her voice. "A fawn."

He moved to stand beside Meri. And just as she'd said, there was a deer standing like a brown slash among the green foliage. The fawn had the speckled back of a youngster, and the relaxed stance of one too new to know the dangers that lurked in the woods. He nosed at the shrubs, nibbling the leafy green delicacies.

"He's so beautiful," Meri said.

"He's too trusting. If he doesn't pay attention, some hunter or a loose dog is going to get him."

She cast a glance at him. "That's pretty pessimistic."

"Realistic, Meri. There's a difference." He nodded toward the window. "I'm surprised you don't have your camera out. You were always taking pictures of this or that when you were younger."

She shrugged. "Let's just enjoy the moment, okay?"

He suspected she was hiding a few secrets in those words, burying a pile of her own regrets beneath that shrug. A different day, a different Jack would have asked, but this Jack had learned to leave well enough alone and not go poking sticks if he didn't want one poked in the embers of his own past.

Meri stayed inside her grandfather's house—banished there by Grandpa Ray, who'd told her that he and Jack had the gutter situation under control—washing the dishes and giving his refrigerator a thorough cleaning.

That's what she'd told herself she was in here to do, but her attention kept straying outside, to where Jack and Grandpa Ray worked with easy camaraderie. Grandpa Ray did most of the talking; Jack did most of the working. Meri noticed how Jack would take care of Grandpa without being obvious, how he'd offer to lift something or grab an extra gutter to carry—"Because I might as well carry two if I'm carrying one"—and how he'd find ways to make Grandpa sit down. Have him crimp the ends or hacksaw the end of a gutter while sitting at a makeshift workbench.

The Jack she had known when she was a teenager had been a wild rebel, ready to take on the world, run from the responsibilities that being a Barlow brought. He'd been everything she hadn't—brave and impulsive. She'd dated him partly because she admired him and wanted just a little of that to rub off, to give her the courage to tell her mother *no*, to walk away from the endless pageants and pressure.

But this Jack, the one changed by war and the military, was more reclusive, less impulsive. He had an edge to him that came with a Do Not Trespass sign. It intrigued her, but also reminded her that she wasn't here to open old wounds.

She finished the kitchen, made up a grocery list of things that were healthier options than most of what Grandpa had in his cabinets, then grabbed her purse. She told herself she was helping Grandpa—not avoiding the camera that still sat in its padded bag, untouched for months. A job at a magazine that she had yet to return to, a career she had abandoned. Every time she thought about raising the lens to her eye, though, a flurry of panic filled her. So she did dishes and cleaned house and made lists.

She came around the side of the house to find Grandpa Ray and Jack sitting on the picnic table, under the shade. "I was going to run to the store to grab some food for you, Grandpa."

"I have food in there."

"Beef jerky is not food. And neither is fake cheese spread."

"What can I say? I keep it simple." Grandpa Ray shrugged. "I cook about as well as a squirrel scuba dives."

She laughed. "Well, I'm here now and I'll cook for you. Healthy stuff that'll make you feel better and get your heart back on track and your cholesterol down. And don't argue with me—I'm determined to sway you to the world of nonfried foods."

"We'll see about that. If you ask me, there isn't one food on God's green earth that isn't improved by some batter and hot oil. While you're there, if it ain't too much trouble, throw an extra rabbit in the pot for this guy." Grandpa Ray threw an arm around Jack's shoulders. "He'll starve to death living on his own. Plus, I owe him at least a meal for helping me today."

"It was nothing, Ray, really." Jack got to his feet. "Anyway, I have to go to the hardware store for a couple more pieces and then we can finish this up. While I'm there, I should pick up some more siding. That whole northern side is rotting away."

"You two should go together. Save some gas." Ray gestured between Meri and Jack and grinned. "Get the two of you out of my hair for a while, too."

"Oh, I'm fine—"

"I'm good—"

"You're both as stubborn as two goats in a pepper patch," Ray said, then he reached forward and plucked Meri's keys out of her hand and tucked them in his pocket. "There. Now you have to go with Jack."

Jack scowled and cursed under his breath. "I gotta measure something first." He stalked over to the make-shift workbench set on two sawhorses, grabbed a piece of gutter and a tape measure, but he moved too fast and the gutter slid through his hand. An ugly red gash erupted on his palm and blood spurted from the wound. He cursed again, pressed the hem of his T-shirt against his palm. "Got any Band-Aids, Ray?"

"Band-Aids? You need a tourniquet. They can see that gusher from Mars, boy. You gotta get someone to look at that."

Jack shook his head. "I'm fine."

Meri knew that stubborn set to Jack's shoulders, the tightening of his brows. He'd probably let his hand succumb to gangrene before he asked for help. She marched over and took his hand in hers before he could protest. "Let me see."

"I'm—"

"Bleeding like a stuck pig. Let me go get some first aid supplies and take care of it for you." She pressed the shirt back down. "Hold this and don't move."

"Yes, ma'am." A grin darted across his face then disappeared just as fast.

The way he said *yes, ma'am* caused a little hitch in her step, a catch in her breath. She forgot all those very good reasons why she wasn't attracted to him anymore. Damn.

She hurried into Grandpa's house, raided his medicine chest for some supplies, then went back outside. True to his word, Jack had stayed in the exact same spot. She uncoiled the hose and brought it over to him, then turned the knob and waited for a steady stream of cool water. "Here. We need to wash it out first."

The instant the water hit his hand, Jack let out a yelp and pulled away. She smirked. "Are you going to tell me that a man who has fought in one of the most dangerous places in the world is afraid of a little water?"

"Hey, it stings like hell."

She made a face at him. "Come on, buttercup, suck it up."

"Okay. Just make it quick and try not to amputate my hand, Florence Nightingale."

She dried his palm with a clean towel, then had Jack hold pressure on the wound. "I'll have you know I got my first aid badge in Girl Scouts. On the second try."

He chuckled. "That gives me comfort."

"I can handle this. But if you break your leg, you're on your own."

"Hey, I can fashion a splint out of two twigs and a piece of ivy, so I should be good to go."

She smiled, looked up at him, and in that moment, they were teenagers sitting by the banks of the creek, and Jack was doing his best to dry her tears and pull off a miracle with a handmade bandage. His hands that day had been careful and steady, the kind that told her anything she put in his grasp would be safe and cared for. "You remember that baby bird?"

A tiny robin that had fallen from its nest. Probably part of its momma's attempt to get her little one to fly, to be independent, but in the process, the tiny thing had injured a wing and flapped in a panicked circle on the ground. Meri had gone to the only person she knew who could make everything right—Jack.

"I remember you finding it, and coming to me with tears streaming down your face, begging me to fix it." He reached up his free hand and brushed a lock of hair away from her forehead. Her skin seemed to melt where he touched her, and she swayed a little in his direction. The world dropped away. All she saw was Jack's blue eyes. All she heard was the steady rise and fall of his breath, the soft murmur of his deep voice. "You were always trying to save lost causes, Meri."

Lost causes. Oh, how she knew about those. She was smarter now, no longer that foolish girl who believed in fairy tales.

"Not anymore," she said, then looked away, back at his hand, blinking away the tears that sprang to her eyes. She cleared her throat, then pulled the rag from his hand to squeeze a little antibiotic cream on the wound. "Stay still, Jack."

His large, strong hand was warm against hers, solid.

She wanted to study the lines and muscles, to feel the touch of those confident palms against her skin. A long time ago, Jack's hands had touched her, made her sigh and moan and almost want to cry with anticipation. Damn. All that from a memory of a wounded baby bird?

"Uh...let me put a couple bandages on this. With some, um..." She held up the supplies beside her. "Um..."

"Tape?"

"Yeah, tape." She pressed a gauze pad onto his wound, then let go of his hand to tear off long strips of tape. She wrapped them around to the back of his hand, crisscrossing the gauze to hold it in place. "There you go. Almost as good as new."

"I'll never be good as new again. Too many scars." He had a smile on his face, but it didn't hold in his eyes, and for the hundredth time since she'd run into him, Meri saw that other edge to Jack, the edge that she didn't know, or recognize.

"We should get to the store," she said, releasing his hand and gathering the supplies before she gave in to the temptation to ask Jack what was brewing behind those blue eyes and why she cared so much. "Before anyone gets hurt again."

Chapter Four

Kicking and screaming. That was how he went into Doc Malloy's office. On their way into town, Jack had told Meri he was fine, damn it, just fine, but she'd seen the blood seeping through the bandage and insisted he needed stitches. He'd told her it wasn't anything a couple butterfly bandages couldn't fix, and she'd just given him that look of hers.

That look where her eyes narrowed and her lips pursed and one eyebrow arched. He'd wanted to laugh, to tell her that it didn't work anymore, but then the light in her green eyes flickered, and for a second he thought maybe she was worried about him.

"Come on," Meri said, when she returned to the truck. "I checked with his receptionist and she said there's no wait."

"I'm fine, Meri."

She gave him the look again, then grabbed the sleeve of his shirt and tugged him out of the truck and up the walkway into Doc Malloy's office. "Let the professional decide that."

Jack paused a moment in the doorway, waiting for his eyes to adjust to the dim interior. Meri had released him, and stepped two steps to the left. For some reason he refused to decipher, a little shiver of disappointment ran through him when she did that.

"Jack Barlow. Always a pleasure to see you, *sugar.*" Corinna Winslow's voice came across the room like warm honey. She slipped out from behind the reception desk and sashayed across the small room. Corinna had been a cheerleader in high school, and even back then, she had pursued Jack with single-minded determination. They'd gone on a couple dates, years ago, but Jack had little interest in Corinna and had put a quick end to it. When he'd come home, she'd been one of the first to call to see if he "needed anything. Anything at all."

Now she put a palm on his chest, just a light, quick touch, but one that seemed to stamp him. "Don't tell me you're hurt."

He held up his hand. "Nothing big. I figured I could get by with some bandages, but someone—" he jerked his head in Meri's direction but she just gave him that look again "—insisted on stitches."

Corinna took Jack's injured hand in hers. "Oh, my. Yes, stitches indeed. Let me take you right back, sugar, and get you all fixed up."

Before he could protest, Corinna was leading him down the hall and into an exam room. What was with the women in his life today? Herding him around like a wayward sheep, for God's sake.

Corinna leaned in as she took his blood pressure and temperature—two things Jack was sure he didn't need—but Corinna insisted. She wore a snug-fitting V-necked white T-shirt under an unbuttoned scrubs top, which meant he got more than one healthy look at her cleavage. Jack was pretty sure nurses weren't supposed to bend like that to take a blood pressure, but he didn't argue.

On any other day, he would have enjoyed the obvious flirtation. Maybe even traded a few innuendos with Corinna, who had never made a secret of her interest in him. Instead, he found himself wondering about Meri, sitting in the uncomfortable chair in the waiting room. Not just wondering about what her cleavage looked like—hell, he wasn't dead, after all—but what he had seen in her eyes earlier today when she'd seen the vulnerable, determined fawn.

And why he still cared.

He, of everyone in the world, should stay far, far away from Meri Prescott. Not just because he had already learned his lesson about tangling with a woman who lived in that world of debutantes and beauty pageants, of hair spray and high heels. Once upon a time, that hadn't bothered him. Then he'd gone to war and become a different man. Not a better man, some would argue.

And then there was Eli. Just those three letters sent a sharp pain searing through his chest.

"You okay?" Corinna asked.

He jerked his attention back. "Uh, yeah. The stethoscope was a little cold."

"Oh, don't tell me you can't take a little cold, a big, strong man like yourself." She gave him a playful swat. "Or, I can warm it up against my own skin first. If you'd like."

Before she could do that—and Jack really didn't want to know where the stethoscope was going to get warmed—the door opened and Doc Malloy came in. Corinna stepped back, fumbling with the blood pressure cuff.

"Why, hello, Jack," the doctor said. "Haven't seen you in a long time."

Jack leaned forward and shook hands with the elderly doctor. He'd known Doc Malloy all his life, and except for a few more pounds around his gut and a few more white hairs on top of his head, the doctor looked about the same as he had when he'd given Jack his first vaccination shots. He was an amiable doctor, one often given to long chats with patients he knew well. Doc had fought in Vietnam, and had traded a few war stories with Jack over the years. "Nice to see you again, sir."

Doc Malloy nodded at Jack's bandaged hand. "What seems to be the trouble?"

"Just a little flesh wound. Meri thought—"

"Meri Prescott? She's back in town?"

Jack nodded. God, he hoped they didn't get into a lengthy conversation about Meri. He didn't want to think about her any more than was necessary, and over the last day, that had been like every five seconds. "She thought I needed stitches."

"If there's one thing I've learned in thirty years of marriage, it's that the woman is always right." Doc Malloy grinned. "And even when you think she's wrong, you agree anyway. Happy wife makes for a happy life."

"Uh, Meri and I aren't…she isn't…" What was with him? Since when did he stumble and stutter? "She's just visiting her grandpa."

Across the room, Corinna's face broke into a smile.

She fiddled with the chart, but kept a pair of coquettish eyes on Jack's face.

Doc Malloy bent to study Jack's injury. In the end, he decided a few stitches were called for, after all. Corinna stayed by the doc's side, handing him supplies, but keeping her attention on Jack. She'd flash him a smile from time to time, when she wasn't contorting herself to give him a direct view of her best assets. Once Jack's hand was bandaged, Corrina ducked out, with a little sashay, to refill the supplies.

"There you go, good as new," Doc Malloy said.

It was almost the same thing Meri had said earlier. Did people really think a bandage or two would change anything about Jack?

"I've been so battered and bruised in the last year, Doc, I'll never be good as new." It wasn't just what had happened to Jack on the outside—those scars had healed, faded to almost nothing—it was the burdens he carried inside his heart, the guilt that weighed down his every step, like an elephant hanging off his heel.

Jack was the one who could sit out on his back porch and look across beautiful Stone Gap Lake, soaking up the warmth of the sun, breathing in the fresh, clean air. Eli never would again. Would never know those joys or moments of peace. Because of Jack's decisions, Jack's choices, Jack's *mistakes*.

Doc Malloy laid a hand on Jack's arm and met his gaze. "You know how they temper steel? They take it to its limit over and over again, then let it cool, until it becomes so hardened and strong there's almost nothing that can break it or change it. That's how people get tempered, too. They get broken, they go through tragedies, triumphs, pain, loss, new lives being born and others lost to death." The kindly doctor's eyes met Jack's with a knowledge that came from years of continuity. Doc had given Jack his kindergarten polio vaccine and his last checkup before he shipped off to boot camp. Doc's blue eyes were eyes that knew Jack, knew him as much more than another file in the cabinet. "The hells people go through make them stronger in the end, stronger than steel."

Jack lifted his newly bandaged hand and cradled it in the opposite palm. There was no bandage to fix what was wrong with Jack inside his soul. "Sometimes the tests go too far, the heat too great, and they break."

"The people? Or the steel?"

"Doesn't matter, Doc. Does it?" Jack slipped off the table and headed for the door. "Thanks again for fixing me up."

"I only fix the outside problems, Jack. A man's gotta fix the inside ones on his own."

Jack just nodded to that and headed out to the waiting room.

Meri was reading a magazine when Jack entered the room, her blond head bent over the glossy pages. The sun streamed in through the window behind her. Like a halo, he'd say, if he was a sentimental guy.

She looked up and a smile curved across her face, and something caught in his chest, something that fluttered like hope, that made him feel like the kid he used to be a long time ago. Then the smile was gone and she was all business, putting the magazine to the side and fishing her keys out of her purse. "All set?"

"Yup." He paid the bill, then the two of them walked back into the bright sunshine. Meri unlocked the truck and climbed in the driver's seat, waiting for him to get in on the other side. Without a word, she put the truck in gear and traveled the mile to the hardware store. Jack glanced over at her, but she kept her gaze on the road. He told himself he was glad.

The air between them chilled, and the silence thickened the air in the truck. When he unconsciously reached for the door handle with his right hand, he winced when the newly bandaged injury let out a protest.

"You okay?" Meri asked. *"Sugar?"*

"Is that jealousy I hear in your voice?"

"I'm not jealous of anyone. And especially not of that plastic enhanced former cheerleader."

He arched a brow. "Are you sure about that? Because it sounds like you might want to go back in there and stick her stethoscope in a painful place."

Meri waved toward the hardware store. "Why don't you go get what you need, and I'll hit the grocery store. Kill two birds with one stone."

On any other day, Jack would have welcomed the opportunity to be alone, puttering around among tools and nuts and bolts. But instead, he found himself raising the bandaged hand and giving Meri a pity-me smile. "I'm, uh, not so sure I should be lifting tools and plywood with this. I could open the stitches up. That could lead to an infection. Gangrene. Amputation."

She shook her head and laughed. "Has anyone ever told you that you're a drama queen?"

"I'm just trying to head off further injuries." He worked up the pity-me smile again. "If you suffer through the hardware store with me, I promise not to complain when we're picking out cereal at the Sav-a-Lot."

She shifted in the seat and narrowed her gaze. "Your hand hurts that much?"

"Oh, it was a really deep cut. Doc Malloy said I almost severed a nerve." Okay, so he hadn't said any such thing, but Jack figured telling a white lie to garner a little sympathy from Meri wasn't a bad thing.

"Okay. But only if you promise one thing." She wagged a finger at his chest. "You won't spend an hour in the power tool section, drooling like a five-year-old in the candy aisle."

He caught her finger with his good hand. "I promise not to spend an hour in the power tool section. But I don't promise not to drool."

At least over the tools. Right now, with her hair loose around her shoulders and those faded denim shorts hugging her thighs, he couldn't promise not to drool over Meri. Seemed his hormones kept forgetting his brain's resolve to stay far, far away from her.

"It's a good thing Nurse Sugar made sure you had plenty of bandages on your hand, should you need to wipe your chin." Meri slid her finger out of his grasp, then stepped out of the truck and marched into the hardware store before he could even open his door.

Jack chuckled. Seemed Corinna's flirting had lit a fire under his old flame. For a second he wanted to explore that spark, see where it led. To touch more than a single digit on Meri's hand, to explore more than just the look in her eyes.

The glass door shut behind Meri's curvy hips, and Jack's reflection shimmered before him. He had a day's worth of stubble on his chin, a tear in the neck of the faded T-shirt he was wearing, and a hole in the knee of his jeans. But like Doc Malloy had said, those outside imperfections were temporal, a mask for the damages underneath.

He closed his eyes for a second, and in his mind he was back on the battlefield, surrounded by dust and diesel fumes and frustration. He could hear the rumble of the engines, the *whoop-whoop-whoop* of the helicopters above them, and the frightened cries of the wounded. And he saw himself, standing there for a moment, just like he was now, his reflection shimmering in the panel of the Humvee, its back half still sitting as pristine as if it had just been driven off some car lot, while the front driver's side was gone, erased with a blast.

"Jack?"

His mind was caught in a tumbling wave, spiraling backward, drowning, dark, as if he couldn't find the surface.

"Jack?"

Then a soft touch on his arm. He jumped, adrenaline shooting through his veins, then his mind caught up with his eyes and his heartbeat slowed, one beat at a time. "Sorry. I was…daydreaming."

More like having a waking nightmare, but Jack didn't want to talk about that. Not with Meri, not with Doc Malloy, not with anyone.

"Are you okay? You look a little pale."

"I'm fine," he barked. "Now let me get what I need here so I can get back to work. I don't have all day to stand around and jabber." He brushed past her and into the store, knowing he was being an ass and not caring. Because caring would mean explaining, and he sure as hell wasn't doing that.

She lingered at the back of the store while he grabbed a cart and filled it with the supplies he needed. By the time he reached the checkout counter, guilt weighed on his shoulders. None of this was Meri's fault. Taking it out on her, simply because she reminded him of his mistakes, was wrong. .

Jack shoved the change in his pocket, then wheeled the cart over to Meri. "Sorry for biting your head off."

"Thank you for apologizing." A smile curved across her face, easing from appreciation to a tease. "But don't think I won't make you pay for that."

The way she looked at him, with that light in her eyes, pushed away the dusty, desolate world of Afghanistan. The weight in his chest eased slightly and for a moment, he was an ordinary man out with an ordinary woman.

He arched a brow. "Pay? How?"

A twinkle danced in her eyes and made something in his stomach flip. "I'm gonna take a very, very long time deciding between Froot Loops and Apple Jacks."

The tension from earlier slid away like water running down Jack's back. He couldn't remember the last time he had felt like this, as if the only thing he had to worry about was how long it took to buy groceries. Maybe Meri returning to town wasn't such a bad thing, after all. "You say that like it's an actual choice."

"It is." She lowered her nose and gave him a piercing stare. "I take my cereal very, very seriously, Jack Barlow."

Damn, he liked the way she said his name. "Anyone who takes their cereal seriously knows that Froot Loops are better than Apple Jacks."

"Oh, yeah? You want to put a wager on that, Mr. Barlow?"

"First off," he said, taking a step closer to her, until mere inches separated them, until he could catch the dark floral notes of her perfume and see the gold flecks in her green eyes, "since when do you call me Mr. Barlow?"

She opened her mouth to speak. The tease had disappeared from her eyes, replaced by something he couldn't read. "Since we haven't been familiar in a long time."

"I'd say we're pretty familiar right now." Given how close they were, given how much he wanted to kiss her. "We are, after all, discussing breakfast. That's something I usually don't do until after the third date. So what do you say? Want to have a bowl of Fruit Loops with me? We'll settle this debate once and for all."

Was he really asking her to choose the best cereal? Or for something more?

She put a hand on his chest, a flutter of a touch that made his heart stutter, then turned on her heel. "Discussing breakfast and having it together are two very, very different things, *Mr.* Barlow."

For a little while, Meri had forgotten the scar on her face. For some reason, whenever she was with Jack, it was as if that scar didn't exist. Maybe because he never stared at it as if the crescent shape was a blinking red light. Maybe it was because seeing Jack made her feel as if she was sixteen again, way before she'd left Stone Gap. Way before she'd found a new life in New York, and way before the moment that had changed her in fundamental ways.

Then Meri walked into the Sav-a-Lot and in five seconds, a reminder came rushing over in the form of Esther Klein.

"Oh, my goodness, Meri Prescott! You're back in town." The grocery store owner had her arms outstretched to welcome Meri with a hug. She corralled Meri against her ample chest, then pushed her back. "Lord

Almighty, girl, what happened to you? Were you in an accident?"

"No. I'm fine. It's just a scar from a cut, nothing big." There was no way she wanted to get into the details of what had happened. Given the way gossip spread in Stone Gap, the story would explode like a wildfire by the end of the day.

"But it's…you were so beautiful…" Esther flushed. "I mean, you still are beautiful, of course, but—"

"We better get those groceries," Jack said. He'd grabbed a cart from the corral at the front of the store and handed it off to her. "Your grandpa is waiting on us."

"So nice to see you again, Mrs. Klein," Meri said, then headed down the aisle with Jack before Esther could finish what came after the *but*. Meri had heard it all before. *But now you're so different. But now your face is forever changed. But now no one here will ever see you the same as they did before.*

All her life, Meri had thought she wasn't vain, that she didn't give a damn what anyone thought about her looks. But when she saw that mixture of horror and pity in Esther's eyes—and so many like her—Meri realized she was lying to herself. She did care. The identity she had despised—the beauty queen—was forever altered, and that made Meri wonder what identity the scar raised. The scared woman who couldn't face the city or her camera again? Or a woman who had survived, and would persevere again? Or would that scar win in the end?

Her hand went to her cheek. She hooked a hank of her hair and brought it forward over her cheek to cover the scar.

Jack stopped the cart. "Don't."

"Don't what?"

"Don't cover that up just because some brain-dead woman made a senseless comment." He reached over and brushed her hair behind her ear again. "You have nothing to be embarrassed about."

Meri shook her head. "I'm not who I used to be, and people in this town are never going to get past that."

"Well, then, they're just ignorant. Don't they realize you're too damned smart to be prancing down a runway in a tiara?"

She laughed. "Gee, thanks."

"It's true. You're too smart to be just a beauty queen and too beautiful to let the pettiness of someone who should know better than to run their mouth bother you."

Jack calling her beautiful touched her more than she realized. Even with the scar, even with a few more years behind her? Or was he just being polite? She cocked a grin at him. "Are you complimenting me, Jack Barlow?"

"Hell, no. Gentlemen compliment women, and I am no gentleman." He gave his head a mock toss, which made her laugh, and then he gestured toward their empty cart. "Now let's get this grocery store torture over with."

"Thank you."

He shrugged. "No need to thank me. I know what it's like to have people asking a lot of nosy questions."

She wanted to ask what he meant. Was it the war? The loss of Eli? The difficulty in coming back to Stone Gap? But then she realized she would be doing the very thing they both hated—asking a lot of nosy questions. So instead, she headed the cart down the bread aisle. To, as Jack had said, get this grocery torture over with.

The store was relatively empty, caught in that midday window of too late for the lunch-hour shopping trips and too early for the after-school dinner rush. Meri reached for a loaf of wheat bread and dropped it into the top basket of the cart.

"If that's for Ray, he's not going to eat it. He claims he's allergic to fiber."

Meri raised a doubting brow. "*Allergic* to fiber?"

"Ever since he heard about people going gluten-free, he's been staging a one-man protest against wheat, cruciferous vegetables and low-fat margarine."

"In favor of the crap he normally eats?"

"Hey, I eat the same crap." Jack grinned.

"Exactly why I'm buying this. And this one, too." She tucked a second loaf into the cart. Jack mounted a protest, but she ignored him and headed for the vegetable aisle. "And some broccoli."

Behind her, Jack groaned. She just laughed and kept going.

It was easier to tease him with dark leafy greens than to deal with whatever had been between them earlier. The second he'd closed the gap between them and touched her cheek, her heart had tripped, and she'd been sixteen again, standing in that garage, thinking there was no one in the world she'd ever love as much as she loved Jack Barlow. Then he'd broken her heart and she'd vowed to never, ever let anyone get that close.

When he'd brushed her hair back behind her ear and told her she was beautiful, she had forgotten about that day in the garage. Forgotten about her promise to herself. She'd thought about him kissing her—did she want him to kiss her? How would it be, after so many years? Better? Sweeter?

"Uh…zucchini or summer squash?" she asked Jack, if only to think about something other than his lips on hers.

"Zucchini. Sauté it with a little garlic and a dash of dill, and it brings out the flavor without all the sodium."

She slid three zucchinis into a plastic bag, then turned to Jack. "You cook? Since when?"

"I do a lot of things you don't know about," he said.

"Me, too." She shrugged. "I guess we both grew up a lot in the last few years."

"More than you know." His voice was low, quiet.

Again, another statement that invited questions. Questions she didn't ask. "Fuji or Gala apples?"

"I'm more of a Granny Smith guy. Ray likes Red Delicious."

"How do you know so much about what my grandfather likes to eat?"

Jack shrugged, and avoided her gaze while he added a few apples to a bag and put them in the cart. "I've done his shopping for him for a while now."

"You have?"

Another shrug. "He hasn't been feeling well for a long time, Meri. And there was a time…" Jack cleared his throat. "Anyway, he's getting better now, and that's what matters."

"What aren't you telling me?"

Jack didn't say anything for a long time. So long she began to wonder if he was going to answer her at all. "I really think it's a good thing you're home now. Ray isn't the most compliant with doctors' orders. It'll be harder for him to sneak in a box of Twinkies with both of us watching over him."

He said it with a light tone, as if things weren't all that serious. As if they didn't have a thing to worry about as long as Grandpa chose wheat over white. But she read the unspoken message underlying Jack's words—Grandpa's health was still teetering on a dangerous edge. Aunt Betty tried, but Grandpa Ray had always kept his distance from Anna Lee's side of the family, especially after his son had died. But he'd always treated Meri, Eli and Jack like his own children, which was probably why Jack saw him as family, not just a friend.

Meri had seen the row of heart medications on Grandpa Ray's counter. His heart was weak, and as he edged toward eighty-five, there was no chance of it getting stronger. If Grandpa Ray watched his health and took better care of himself, he would be here a good long while yet. Meri needed him still, needed his wisdom and his gentle love. Just the thought of losing Grandpa, so close in the wake of losing Eli—

"Do you think it's because of Eli?" she asked. "Maybe Grandpa was more upset about that than he let on. Eli was like a son to him, you know."

"You think I forgot about that? I know what Eli meant to him." Jack turned away and started stuffing peppers into a bag. One, two, three, four.

Meri laid a hand on his, just for a second, then withdrew. "You okay?"

"I'm just buying peppers."

Five, six, seven.

"Um, I don't think we need that many peppers. I don't even know what to do with that many."

He let out a long breath, as if he was pulling it from a well deep in his gut, then withdrew three of the peppers, twisted the top of the bag and fashioned a knot. He moved on to the tomatoes. She let him go. Watched him fill a bag with tomatoes, another with cucumbers, a third with onions.

Jack Barlow was building a No Trespassing sign out

of vegetables. And Meri Prescott, who had a few of those signs around herself, wasn't about to cross the line. By the time they moved on, the cart was filled with enough vegetables to feed a small town in Ethiopia.

"Are we done?" Jack asked. His tone had shifted and whatever storm had been in him earlier seemed to have abated.

"Almost. Can't forget cream for my coffee." She swung the cart down the dairy aisle, opened one of the refrigerated cases and withdrew a pint of half-and-half for herself, a fat-free one for Grandpa Ray.

He scoffed. "Now that's something I never thought I'd see."

"What?"

"The Meri I knew drank her coffee and her tea black. Never used salad dressing, butter, or had dessert."

"That Meri..." She let out a breath and debated how much to tell him, standing here between the sour cream and cottage cheese. "That Meri was someone else's creation."

"And what about this Meri?"

"This one is all mine, faults and all."

He shifted closer to her. The refrigerators hummed softly beside them. A tinny, distant voice called for a cleanup in aisle three over the tacky notes of the Muzak on the sound system. "From where I'm standing," Jack said quietly, "there aren't any faults at all."

She glanced away, caught her reflection in the glass doors, then dropped her gaze to the scuffed tiles. "You don't know me anymore, Jack."

"I have known you since you were old enough to catch frogs in Skinner's Pond, Meri. Since the day you showed up in my backyard with scuffed knees and one missing shoe. Since—"

"Since the day you told me you wanted a woman who worried about more than what she was wearing and how her hair looked."

He winced. "I was young then. And stupid."

She raised her chin. "And what's changed since then?"

He cocked a messy grin. "I'm not young anymore."

Damn him for making her laugh. For making her hate him and forgive him, all in the same breath. If there was one thing that truly hadn't changed since the old days, it was that a part of her heart was still in Jack Barlow's hands.

And that was the one thing she hadn't counted on when she'd returned to Stone Gap.

Chapter Five

Ray sat back in the chrome-and-vinyl chair and patted his belly. "Merry Girl, I have to say, you are the best damned cook in the Prescott family."

Jack was inclined to agree. Meri had made enough to feed a horde of thousands, and like the man-pigs they were, he and Ray had tanked most of the roast turkey, steamed broccoli and sautéed carrots she'd arranged on a platter. Even the salad had been decimated, mostly by Meri and Jack, but Ray had dished up a healthy portion of his own. For a man who normally drew a hex around anything vegetable, he sure had gotten his fill of cruciferous today.

"Thanks, Grandpa." She smiled and got to her feet, reaching for Ray's plate.

"Now, now, let me help you." Ray started to rise but Meri put a hand on his shoulder.

"Stay right where you are, Grandpa. I'm here to take care of you, not the opposite."

Ray leaned back again and crossed his arms over his chest. "A man could sure get used to this life of sloth. Before you know it, I'll be wearing my slippers all damned day and watching Pat Sajak."

"You deserve to do that, Grandpa." She kept her hand resting in a light, tender touch on his shoulder. "You've worked hard all your life."

Ray's work-worn hand covered Meri's and the smile on his face wobbled. "I think you got the best of all the Prescott genes, sweetheart."

Jack had to look away. For God's sake, what the hell was wrong with him? He'd never been an emotional guy. Now he was all choked up, like some hormonal teenager watching a coffee commercial at Christmas. Meri gave her grandfather a soft kiss, then started clearing the table.

Jack jerked to his feet, gathered up the dishes and followed Meri to the kitchen counter. He started the water and loaded the empty plates into the sink, then squirted some dish liquid over them. He told himself the actions would keep him from thinking, from dwelling.

But his brain reached back to the sight of Ray's hand on top of Meri's, and in his head, he saw another moment, another hand reaching for his own. In that instant, there was sand beneath Jack's feet, the pungent smell of gasoline and the sickening stench of charred flesh hanging heavy in the air.

Don't leave me, man. Don't let me die. Eli's words, sounding empty and slow above the hollowness in Jack's ears, as if Eli was yelling down a long, long tunnel.

I won't. I swear to God, Eli, you're not going to die. It was a lie, and Jack had known it, but still he'd refused to believe it. There wasn't enough of Eli's body left to save—most of it lost to the twisted, mangled wreckage that had severed him as easily as cutting a ribbon.

Eli's eyes, wide with terror, and Jack screaming for help, for someone to do something, praying for a miracle in the middle of nowhere. The others in the convoy, littering the ground among them, and Jack trying not to notice one of Eli's legs sitting four feet away, as if it were waiting for him to just pick it up and put it back on. The tourniquets Jack had fashioned on Eli's thighs doing little more than holding on. Then the worst moment of all, when the terror ebbed away and a strange complacency slackened Eli's features.

Tell them I'm sorry. Tell my parents I love...

"Hey, Jack, you trying to start a flood?"

Jack jerked his attention to Meri's voice. He shook off the visions, tried to reorient himself. But his mind stayed back in the desert, back with Eli, back with that last horrible, agonizing, powerless moment.

"Sorry. I...uh...got a little distracted." He shut off the water and plunged the sponge into the sink. Cold. Damn. He emptied the sink and refilled it with hot water. His heart thudded in his chest, his throat seemed to be clogged, and he couldn't think.

"Having some trouble with domestic duties?" She gave him a teasing smile.

"Yeah." Better her thinking that than knowing Jack's real problem was in his head and had been in his head for nearly a year now. It was the one thing he couldn't fix no matter how hard he tried. The one thing they couldn't medicate or bandage or amputate. He'd had a few cuts and scrapes after THAT DAY, but nothing that hadn't healed. Externally.

On the outside, he looked the same as always. Maybe a little less trim than the day he enlisted, but the same. Inside, though, he was a scrambled yowling mess, like a crate of feral cats.

He gave Meri a grin he didn't feel. "You know men. We like to pretend we know it all."

"Here, let me." She slid into place in front of him, and for five seconds, he stayed where he was, with the fresh, light scent of her perfume wafting up to tease his senses. The warmth of her body inches from his. Meri Prescott, the woman he had never really forgotten, standing so close, he'd only have to shift his weight to touch her again.

And where would that get him? Nowhere he could go, that was for damned sure. He'd learned his lesson in the few times he'd tried to date since he got home. Women in relationships wanted to *know*. They wanted to *ask questions*.

Meri, of all people, would want to know everything. Once she realized he'd been with Eli...

Getting close to Meri would mean talking about THAT DAY.

Telling her how he had watched the light and life slowly ebb from Eli's eyes. How he had held Meri's cousin's hand and lied about saving him and protecting him and being the friend he was supposed to be. How at the moment when Eli needed him most, Jack hadn't been there.

"Hey, remember that time Eli twisted a rubber band around the sprayer?" Ray said. "He talked you into getting him a glass of water and damned near busted a gut when that sprayer soaked you, Jack."

Meri laughed. "I remember that. Eli would get that

little devilish look in his eyes and you knew he had a prank waiting for some poor soul."

"God, that boy made me laugh." Ray shook his head.

Jack gripped the edge of the sink, fighting the urge to tell them all to stop talking, to stop mentioning Eli's name. Hearing it was like drowning an open wound in bleach.

"Remember that April Fools' Day when he put that rubber snake—"

"In the toilet," Ray finished for Meri. He laughed for a long time, then sobered and dropped his gaze. "Lord, do I miss that kid. It's a damned shame what happened to him over there. War is a terrible thing. A terrible, terrible thing."

The air thickened. Jack's chest constricted and his heart began to race. Sweat beaded on his brow and he clawed at the top of his T-shirt, as if the soft cotton was a boa constrictor.

"I gotta go clean up outside," Jack said. "It's getting near dark."

He bolted out the back door and stumbled down the three steps that led to the yard. He stood there, bent over, fighting the urge to heave up his dinner, and drawing in deep of the warm, thick air.

His heart slammed against his chest as if it was trying to bust through the walls around it and leap from the cold prison of Jack's body. His throat tightened and the world darkened. He gripped his knees, struggling for air, for clarity, for…reality. Focusing on the details, just like the doctor had taught him to do.

Thick green blades of grass. A smooth gray stone, no bigger than a quarter. A stray nail, rusted and bent, forgotten long ago.

"Jack?"

Thick green blades of grass. A smooth gray stone, no bigger than a quarter. A stray—

"Jack, you okay?" A hand on his back.

He tensed, his fists curling at his sides, his instincts screaming at him to fend off the danger, save the others, *do something, soldier.*

He took a breath, another. Focused on the thick green blades of grass. The touch lingered, innocent, worried, and after a long, long moment, Jack's fists uncurled and the tension eased a notch. "I'm…I'm fine."

He straightened and noticed Meri staring at him. "No, you're not."

"I'm fine, Meri." Maybe if he said it enough, he'd believe it, too.

"You're not fine." Her green eyes were dark pools in the night, catching the moon and reflecting it like diamonds on the water. "Talk to me."

"I don't want to talk about it. Not with you or anyone else." Hadn't he talked enough to that damned psychologist? And where had it gotten him? "I said I'm fine, let it go."

She blew out a breath and propped her hands on her hips. "Okay, if you say you're fine, then you are. But if you ever want to talk, I'm here."

She started to turn away. He didn't think, he just reached for her, catching her arm and spinning her back toward him. Maybe it was the dark. Maybe it was the sound of the water lapping against the banks of the lake. Maybe it was the waking nightmare she'd dragged him out of. But the tides inside of Jack shifted, and needed more of whatever it was that he seemed to feel every time Meri was near.

She let out a little gasp. Her eyes widened. Her pulse ticked in her throat. But she didn't back away. She just held his gaze and waited.

This wasn't the Meri he remembered. The girl who had been too scared to stand up to her demanding mother, the girl who had trotted across stage after stage like a blue-ribbon colt, as perfect as a porcelain doll.

This Meri stood tall and firm, never flinching. He reached up and cupped her jaw, letting his thumb trace along the crescent scar that creased her perfect face. "What happened to you, Meri?"

"Nothing I couldn't handle."

"Is that why you're back here? Because you handled it so well in New York?"

"I'm here…" Her gaze went to the lake, to something far beyond him. "To figure out where to go next."

"You and me both." He had a stack of discharge papers and a pile of medals he didn't want, and no freaking idea what he was going to do tomorrow or the next day or the day after that.

"What do you want, Jack?" she asked, her breath warming the space between them.

"I want…" His gaze dropped to her lips, to the way they parted softly when she let out a breath.

He shifted closer, his hands going up to tangle in her long blond hair. He stopped thinking, stopped second-guessing himself and kissed her. This wasn't the kind of kiss he'd given her all those years ago, both of them young and inexperienced, clumsy and unsure. Those kisses had been sweet, almost chaste compared to this one.

This kiss exploded, a hot, rushed frenzy, his mouth sliding over hers, his tongue darting into her mouth, hungry, needy, wanting and seeking something he'd seen in her eyes, something he had lost a long time ago. Then Meri opened against him with a soft mew, and he nearly came undone.

Then just as quickly, he jerked himself back to reality. This was *Meri*. The last woman on the planet he needed to kiss, to get close to again. Meri, who loved her grandfather and her cousin with a fierceness that most people never got to experience—

Meri, who would never forgive Jack for what he had done.

Jack stumbled back, away from her. "I'm sorry, Meri. Just…stay away from me."

Confusion muddled her eyes. "What…what do you mean?"

"I mean stay the hell away from me. I'm not the man I used to be. And I'm sure as hell not the man you want me to be."

Then he stalked away, climbed into his truck and pulled out of the driveway, before he could do something even more stupid. Like change his mind and finish what he'd started.

The morning dawned, slow and easy, like a cat stretching after a long nap. Meri lay in the unfamiliar bed of the guest cottage, listening to the sounds of the lake waking up outside her open window. Birds calling to each other, boats puttering away from docks, a dog barking after a squirrel or rabbit. It was a song, she thought, a different, softer tune than the one she'd heard in New York, but still a song close to her heart.

How she loved this cabin. This escape from her mother. It was as if Grandpa Ray lived on the other side of the moon. Here, there'd never been a reminder to watch what she ate, an admonishment not to leave her room without her hair and makeup done, or a disapproving stare when she forgot to straighten her spine. Here, she was just...

Meri. She could swim until dark, eat candy for breakfast, wear yesterday's grass-stained shorts with a torn T-shirt. She closed her eyes, snuggling deeper under the cotton duvet. Five more minutes and then she'd go get a cup of coffee and rustle up something for breakfast.

The song of the lake was broken by short, staccato sounds. *Whoosh-thwap-thud.* A curse. Then another *whoosh-thwap-thud.*

Meri swung her legs over the side of the bed, wriggled into a pair of shorts and straightened the T she had worn to sleep. She padded out to the kitchen, which in this cozy cabin was really just a glorified extension of the bedroom, stopped to snag a cup of coffee and add some half-and-half to the brew, and then stepped onto the back porch.

Jack stood in the center of the yard, working up a sweat with a growing pile of wood. After all the wood he had chopped the other day, it looked as though he was getting Ray set for the next decade of cold snaps. Jack set a new log on top of an overturned stump, raised his ax, then swung it forward in one powerful swoop. Two chunks of wood toppled to the grass below. Jack bent, grabbed another log, then paused when he saw Meri. "Mornin'."

Damn, he looked good. Manly and strong and sexy as hell with that ax in one hand and the fine sheen making his suntanned biceps glisten. She thought of that kiss— hell, not a kiss, more of a small nuclear bomb between them—yesterday. Why had he cut it off and disappeared right after? And why had she dreamed about him, about finishing that kiss in her bedroom?

She gripped her coffee mug tighter. "Do you, uh, always start work this early?"

"Early?" He glanced at his watch. "It's half-past nine."

"On a Sunday. Don't you sleep in on Sundays?"

"Don't you get all gussied up to sit on a hard wooden pew and repent for your sins?"

"Only if I have sins to repent for." She gave him a grin and took a step closer, resisting the urge to run her hand along his arm, to feel that hard strength beneath her palm. "Maybe you should go. Though they might need to extend the service for you."

"Oh, really?" He set the ax against the stump and shifted toward her, a tease in his eyes, a smile playing on his lips. "Why's that?"

"Because you have an awful lot to atone for, Mr. Barlow. You are—" she let out a breath, and with it, the words she'd been thinking in a soft whisper "—sin on a stick."

He'd been all that and more last night with that kiss. A kiss that had lingered in her mind, like taffy on the roof of her mouth, sweet and bad for her, all at the same time. Jack Barlow had grown up, and so had his kisses, in ways that made her think of dark nights and tangled sheets and climbing on top of him to quench the flames he'd started deep inside her.

Jack shook his head and a shadow dropped over his features. He picked up the ax and swung it into the stump, hard, swift, lodging the metal blade deep in the thick wood. "Atonement." He spat out the word. "Some things can't be atoned for. Or forgiven."

"What do you mean?"

"Nothing." He sank the ax into the stump and let out a curse. "It's too damned hot to work."

Jack ducked under a low-hanging branch, then trundled down the packed-earth path to the edge of the water. What was that about? What had she said that set him off?

Instead of diving into the lake, Jack just stood at the edge of the water, watching a passing boat. Meri waited awhile for him to return, then gave up and went over to Grandpa Ray's. Her coffee was getting cold, anyway.

Grandpa Ray sat at the kitchen table, flipping through a home improvement store advertisement while he nursed a cup of coffee. "I take it you decided to skip making an appearance this morning with the queen?"

Meri refilled her coffee from Grandpa's carafe, added a little of the fat-free half-and-half she'd bought him, then leaned against the counter. "You mean church with my mother?"

"It is her favorite place for showing off her family, after all."

Or used to be, when Meri was young. Her mother would lay out Meri's clothes the night before, always something sedate but stylish, making sure everything from the color of her bra to the style of her shoes matched the carefully created image. Two hours before the service, her mother would start the beautification process. Manicure touched up, hair curled, makeup applied. A light breakfast, enough to keep Meri's stomach from rumbling at an inconvenient time, but not so much that it would add unnecessary calories to a perfect size-two figure. Then sitting there, with her gloved hands in her lap, a twin to her mother's proper posture, attentive and quiet. Never allowed to yawn or fidget, or skip a single moment of greeting the movers and shakers of Stone Gap, as if Meri was an extension of the family's political and business ambitions.

"I was not invited to church, thank God. Apparently this—" she ran the back of her hand along the scar on her cheek "—invites too many questions. And mars the perfection that Anna Lee demands from a Prescott." Meri added a wry smile as if the rejection didn't hurt. As if it didn't bother her one bit that the one person on earth who was supposed to love her no matter what had shunned her daughter once she lost her perfect sheen and her usefulness in the pageant world.

Clearly, Meri had been a fool, thinking her mother would change.

"Forgive me, but your mother is an idiot if she can't see that you are perfect the way you are," Grandpa Ray said. "Hell, you'd be perfect if you had six toes, a giant purple nose and a goiter hanging off the back of your neck."

Meri laughed and gave her grandfather a quick, tight hug. "You always know how to make me feel better."

He raised his cup. "That's my job as chief spoiler for my favorite grandchild."

Meri grabbed the carafe and topped off her grandfather's coffee, then did the few dishes in his sink. The quiet of the lake and the cottage hovered like a blanket. She never remembered it being this quiet here, but then she realized why the silence had taken root.

"It's not the same without Eli, is it?" Meri said softly.

"Nope. And it never will be. That boy brought life to every space he occupied." Grandpa Ray's face got wistful and sad. "Betty and George are doing their best, but I know they're hurting. Losing a child leaves a hole nothing can ever fill."

Meri glanced out the window. The sun cast a perfect golden wash over the deep blue water of Stone Gap Lake, already filling up with boaters and fishermen. Jack stood on the bank, his hands in the pockets of his khaki shorts, his shoulders hunched. "How's Jack handling it?"

"Not too well. I think he feels personally responsible for Eli's death. I don't know what happened over there. Jack won't talk about it. But I know he's been through a lot." Grandpa sighed. "A lot more than either of us knows."

She'd heard that Eli had served with Jack part of the time he'd been overseas. And knowing Jack—the kind of man who took responsibility for a grandfather he wasn't related to, a garage he didn't own and a friend he'd known all his life—she knew he was probably shouldering a lot of grief over the loss of Eli.

Her cousin had been gone for almost a year now, but she still expected to see him loping into the kitchen, helping himself to whatever he could find in Grandpa's fridge. She missed hearing his voice, seeing his goofy grin, and even missed the way he'd tease her, as if she was a pesky tagalong little sister.

"I remember when I came home from the war," Grandpa Ray said. "I was a mess. It was your grand-mother who set me straight. She sat up with me more than one night when I couldn't sleep. For months, I wouldn't talk, wouldn't do anything but sit in front of the damned TV and fester in my own misery. She sat there, every night, waiting, for me to get over myself and let go of the demons in my head."

Meri turned back to her grandfather. "And did you?"

Grandpa Ray wrapped his hands around his coffee mug and stared into the steamy brew. "One night, I sat there so long, the bars and tone came on. This was back in the days when television stations shut down at night, and when they started up again, they put up a picture of the Old Glory and played 'The Star-Spangled Banner.' After my show ended, I sat there through the bars and tone, a half hour of that, maybe even an hour, and your grandma just waited, as patient as a saint. Then the flag appeared, I heard the first few notes of 'Oh, say can you see,' and that was it for me. I started bawling like a baby, thinking of all the friends I had lost, all the mistakes I had made, all the regrets that haunted my nights. It all came out then, every last ugly truth. She listened, God bless her, to every single word. Then she got to her feet, drew me into a hug and held on." His face curved into a smile at the memory. "She didn't let go until the day she died."

Tears brimmed in Meri's eyes. She swiped at them with the back of her hand. Hearing her grandfather talk about his late wife made Meri envious in a way. Someday maybe she'd know a love like that, too. "Aw, Grandpa, that is such a sweet story. Makes me miss Grandma even more."

"She was an incredible woman. Truly one of a kind." Grandpa's gaze shifted to the picture of Grandma that sat atop the small hutch he had built for her as a wedding present decades ago. "Until you came along. You remind me of her in a hundred ways."

"Me? Remind you of Grandma?"

"You're strong like her. And stubborn." He chuckled. "When you love someone, you love them no matter what. Even when they refuse to eat the spinach you made for supper yesterday." He gave her a wink.

Meri pushed off from the counter and wrapped her grandfather in a tight hug. He smelled of fresh soap and warm memories, and she held on to that scent and his broad shoulders for a long time. "Thanks, Grandpa."

"Anytime, sweetheart." He patted her back. "Give Jack some time, Merry Girl. He needs patience, time and someone who is willing to give him that. Someone like your grandma."

Was Grandpa Ray implying that someone should be Meri? She hoped not. Even after that kiss, falling for Jack Barlow—or helping him through his own emotional maze—wasn't in her plans.

"I'm not here for Jack, Grandpa. I'm here for you." And for herself. Maybe here she could finally find what she had lost in New York, what had been taken from her on that dark street. And at the same time, deal with the grief of losing Eli, a loss that had punched a hole in the family. She remembered the phone call from her aunt Betty, the stumbled, sobbing words. The way Meri's heart had stopped and her breath had left her. In that moment, she'd known that nothing would ever be the same again, because the middle leg of the tripod was gone and the stool couldn't stand on its own. "That's all I have energy for right now."

Chapter Six

Jack settled his bill with Ernie Whitman, the owner of the hardware store, then started loading the supplies in the back of the truck. He could have just as easily picked all this up yesterday, or even better, waited to buy the siding, but he'd needed an excuse to get the hell away from that look in Meri's eyes. The one that said she wanted to know what was going on inside him and why he'd damned near bitten her when she tried to make small talk.

Yeah, that look. Not something he wanted to deal with today—hell, any day. So he decided to work instead. Work until he couldn't stand up. Work until the only thing he thought about was climbing into bed and falling asleep. Sleep would elude him, as usual. Or worse, sleep would come and fill his mind with nightmares worse than any horror movie he'd ever seen as a kid.

As Jack reached for a long board, another set of hands

lifted the opposite end and shared the burden. Jack looked up and saw his brother standing there, wearing a faded T-shirt and a pair of khaki shorts. Jack shot him a grin that was half annoyance and half *I'm glad to see you because I'm wallowing again and I hate wallowing.* "Slacking on the day job again? Wait. Do you even have a day job?"

"It's Sunday, Jack. Some people *rest* on Sunday. And some people rest every day. Like me."

"Yeah, well some people don't have a schedule to keep." Jack had never understood how his middle brother could spend his days as aimless as a boat without a rudder. Luke had perfected the art of avoiding work, and still their mother fed him and housed him. "Before I know it, July and August will be here and it'll be too damned hot to work outside." And that would mean too much time inside, thinking. Not something Jack wanted to do.

"It's already too damned hot to work, and it's only June. I vote for taking the day off and going swimming."

"Swimming? I got stuff to do."

"Stuff? What stuff? Dad said he's starting back at the garage in a few days, which means you'll have more time on your hands. Time to do things like swimming instead of slaving away seven days a week."

"Maybe I like working seven days a week."

Luke scoffed. "I think Mama should have had you tested as a child. You are clearly not right in the head."

"Are you going to keep on talking?" Jack scowled. "Because I have stuff—"

"To do. Yeah, yeah, I heard you the first three thousand times." Luke gestured toward the long boards leaning against the cart. "What's all this for?"

"I'm fixing some siding on Ray's house."

"Want a hand? Make up for the one that's got the big boo-boo." Luke grinned and nodded toward Jack's bandage.

"*You* are offering to help *me*?"

"Hey, miracles happen every day," Luke said. "Besides, I don't have anything going on today, and figured I could give you—"

"You have an ulterior motive." Jack leaned in close, and studied his brother's blue eyes. Luke flicked his gaze away. "Don't bother lying. I shared a bedroom with you for fifteen years. I can tell when you're lying. What is it? You need me to cover for you while you take date number four hundred and thirty-two out, and don't want date number four hundred and thirty-one to realize she doesn't hold the key to your heart?"

"No, nothing like that. Though I do reserve the right to use that at a future time." Luke gave his brother a sheepish grin. "Okay, sue me. Mama wants to make sure you're at dinner. No excuses."

"I knew it." Jack jerked up the board and loaded it in himself, then waved off Luke's attempt to help on the next one. "I don't need your help."

"No you don't, you ungrateful caveman. But you're getting it anyway. That way you go to dinner and I, the favorite son, rack up even more brownie points with the parentals." Luke raised his chin with an air of superiority.

"What are you, fifteen?"

"Acting younger only accents my charm."

Jack snorted. "No, it makes you look like a fool. A nonworking, living-off-the-family-dime fool."

"I'm going to ignore that and chalk it up to your never-ending pissed-off mood. Which I am also ignoring, because I'm feeling charitable. It is Sunday, after all." Luke picked up two buckets of stain and laid them beside the wood in the truck. "That's the last of it. Want to ride to-gether? You gotta come back into town for dinner any-way."

"No, I do not want to ride together. The cab's filled up with other supplies. And I definitely don't want to go to dinner."

Luke cupped a hand around his ear. "What's that? You want me to meet you at Ray's and help you out so you're done early enough to shower and look like a respectable human being at dinner? Then you can drive yourself over to Mama's, like the grown-up you are? Sounds like a plan. See you in a few."

Before Jack could protest, Luke, slapped him on the back, hopped in his car and drove away. Jack grumbled to himself, then slipped in behind the wheel of the pickup truck. There were days when he loved his brother, and days when he wished Luke would quit trying to be so damned well-meaning.

Meri picked up the heavy black body of the camera and let it sit in her hand, a dense, familiar weight. Her thumb traced over the different knobs and adjustments, the myriad of buttons that would frame and capture an image. With this camera, a used Nikon she had picked up two years ago in a secondhand electronics shop, she had framed sunsets and cityscapes, old men playing chess in the park and children laughing in the rain. She had seen the best and worst of New York, on sunny days and cloudy days, and had been on her way to having a damned good career, until...

She traced the line running along her cheek. In that instant, she could feel the sharp, quick slice of the knife, the cold air rushing into the gash on her cheek before she realized what had happened. The fear, paralyzing, an icy rush freezing her to the sidewalk for one long minute, then too late, the screams bursting from her lungs and—

Meri put down the camera, frustrated. Even now, three months after the attack, the simple act of holding the Nikon brought her right back to that night. When would she be able to pick up her camera and see the present, not the past?

She walked out of her room and headed out into the bright sunshine. On the far side of the house, Jack and his brother Luke were working on repairing Grandpa Ray's siding. Her grandfather napped in his Adirondack chair, under the shade of an oak tree, with a hardcover thriller open and unread on his lap.

This was what she needed more of. This deep green, perfect…normal. Maybe enough of that and she could lift the camera to her eye again and see something other than the past through that lens.

"Hey, Meri!" Luke raised a hand to greet her. His gaze flicked to the scar, then away. Accepting.

She crossed the lawn to the men. The north side of the house was almost fully encased in new clapboard, giving the old cottage a refreshed, happy exterior. Jack was busy nailing siding onto the house, while Luke stood at the workstation fashioned out of two sawhorses and measured the next piece.

She tried not to stare at Jack's butt as he worked, but damn, he was a good-looking man. Muscular legs, strong, broad shoulders that flexed beneath the tight white cotton of his T-shirt. She cleared her throat and forced her gaze to the siding. "You guys are making good progress. You've almost finished the whole house."

"We have incentive." Luke grinned and leaned toward her and lowered his voice. "Roast beef."

"Roast beef?"

"My mother's making dinner tonight. And *the whole family is invited*." He raised his voice on the last part of the sentence, nodding in Jack's direction. Jack just shot him a glare and went back to work. Luke chuckled and turned back to Meri. "That goes for you and your grandpa, too."

"Oh, I couldn't—"

"She's making apple crumble, too. Fresh from the oven, with a scoop of vanilla ice cream melting on top."

How many times had she eaten at Jack's house when she was younger, and seen a glorious, decadent dessert sitting on the counter? And never had a bite, not so much as a crumb of crust or a fingerful of whipped cream. At the Prescott house, there'd been none of that. Not a cookie jar or an errant chocolate. Anna Lee had run a tight ship, one where nothing fattening existed to tempt or derail Meri's diet. Going to Jack's or Eli's had been like being granted early release from food prison.

Thinking about tonight's dessert made Meri's mouth water. Oh, how she wanted it. Craved it.

Okay, so maybe she was craving something besides the dessert. Like a hunk of the man she had kissed the other day. Being at Jack's mother's house would mean seeing more of Jack—a freshly washed, nicely shaved Jack. "Apple crumble? Oh, Lord. I dream about your mother's desserts sometimes."

"Yup. Plus homemade biscuits, mashed potatoes and the green beans she canned last year, sautéed with a little bacon. It's one giant, glorious heart attack on a plate."

Jack stalked over, grabbed the next piece of siding.

"That's not something Ray should be eating. Or anyone who wants to live past the age of thirty, for that matter."

"Anyone ever tell you that you're a party pooper?" Luke called after his brother, but Jack ignored him. Luke shook his head, cut the next piece of siding with the circular saw, then set it to the side. "Don't tell my father or Mr. Wonderful over there, but my mother switched out the ingredients after Dad's cholesterol got too high. There's turkey bacon in the green beans, and cauliflower mixed in with the potatoes. Mom pretends everything is the same as always, and my dad pretends he doesn't taste the difference."

"It's a marriage based on lies," Jack muttered.

"But it works." Luke turned back to Meri. "So, you in?"

Meri glanced over at her grandfather. It would do him good to get out of the house, to see some people. She had always enjoyed being at Jack's house, with his warm and amiable family. Maybe it would do her some good, too. Help her shake this…cloud. "Sounds wonderful. We'll be there."

Luke thumbed toward Jack. "See if you can convince His Royal Grumpiness to go, too."

"I heard that," Jack said. "His Royal Grumpiness? Really?"

"Good. You were supposed to." Luke grinned. "Hey, I could have called you a royal something else, but I'm trying not to sin. It's Sunday, after all."

Jack rolled his eyes as he took the next piece of siding and went back to work. A smile flickered on his face, though, just before he turned back to hammer the siding onto the house.

"I think I'm winning him over," Luke whispered to Meri.

"Must have been the apple crumble."

"I think it was the guest list." Luke gave her a smile, then bent his head and started measuring the next piece.

"Uh, I don't know about that." Jack had barely looked in her direction today. One would never know they had kissed each other yesterday. Or dated in the past. It was as if she didn't exist.

Her hand drifted up to her cheek and traced along the scar. Was it this? Was Jack so shallow that he couldn't see past the damage to her face?

Either way, she didn't care. She wasn't here to heal a relationship years in the past. She wasn't here to figure out a man who had become an enigma in the years since she left.

Meri headed into the house. She busied herself making a spinach salad with candied pecans and fresh strawberries. She crumbled a little feta cheese over the greens, then whisked together a raspberry vinaigrette, storing it in a squeeze bottle to add at the last minute. She stowed the salad in the fridge for taking to the Barlow house later, then assembled some turkey sandwiches and a pitcher of lemonade. The domestic duties made her feel normal, like any other woman in the South, fixing a side dish for a dinner and making a lunch for the hardworking men in the yard. A thousand miles away from the pampered beauty queen who had been forbidden from so much as pouring herself a glass of milk.

We have help for that, Meredith, her mother would say. *A lady doesn't worry herself with such petty things.*

If her mother could see her now, wearing an apron and carrying a tray laden with sandwiches, an icy pitcher of lemonade and a stack of glasses, Anna Lee would probably faint right there on the spot. When Meri had moved out on her own and into that cramped studio in New York City, she'd realized pretty quickly that she had almost no homemaking skills. She'd burned grilled cheese, shrunk a favorite sweater and clogged the garbage disposal—twice. Despite the bumpy path to domesticity, Meri had loved learning how to fend for herself, how to cook, how to clean. She was no Martha Stewart, but she could make a decent meal and keep a clean house.

Doing those things filled her with an odd sense of accomplishment, as if she had mastered one of the great secrets of life. Clearly, she had been exposed to way too much hair spray as a child.

Meri bumped open the screen door with her hip, then made her way down the stairs and over to the wooden picnic table, still sitting in the same place under the old oak tree. Spanish moss hung like a dreamy curtain and the grass beneath the table had died in a bald oval. Meri set the dishes on the table, then put two fingers in her mouth and let out a short, sharp whistle. "Lunch!"

Grandpa Ray got to his feet, Jack and Luke put down their work, and the three men headed for the table.

"Lunch? Awesome." Luke clapped Meri on the shoulder. "You are an angel, Meri Prescott. Plus one hell of a whistler. Where did you learn to do that?"

"Actually, Jack taught me."

At the mention of his name, Jack raised his head. His blue eyes met hers, and sent a funny little flip through her stomach. Apparently, her stomach hadn't gotten the memo earlier that she wasn't interested in him and didn't care what—or if—he thought about her.

"I remember that day," he said. "God, that was like a million years ago."

"Hey, I'm not that old. I was eight. You were almost eleven." She'd been infatuated from the minute she'd met Jack Barlow, convinced he was the handsomest boy she'd ever seen. With a wide smile, those big blue eyes and a way of wrapping her in a cloud of his charm. He'd been Eli's friend, and she'd been Eli's constant companion, escaping from the suffocating house on Cherrystone Avenue as often as she could with the cousin who often disobeyed Anna Lee's stern rules and took Meri tree climbing and frog hunting. With the boys, Meri could get muddy and scuffed and forget about things like keeping her spine straight when she walked and holding a smile until her teeth felt as though they were going to shatter. Of course, there was always hell to pay when she got home, and eventually she stopped climbing trees and playing in the mud. It was easier to be a bystander, longing for that freedom, than to face the wrath of Anna Lee later.

"You were the annoying tagalong," Jack said. "Always underfoot with us boys."

She parked a fist on her hip. "I was never annoying."

Jack arched a brow.

"Okay, maybe a *little* annoying." The boys had tolerated her because she came as part of the package with Eli. But Jack…Jack had been different. Maybe it was because he had a younger brother or maybe it was because he was the kind of guy who would rescue a baby bird that had tumbled from the nest. She'd found him fascinating, and everything Jack tried, she tried, too, in that backward kind of young love where imitation covered for the nerves of a blooming infatuation.

Jack laid his hammer on the end of the table, then crossed to her. "I distinctly remember telling you to get lost. More than once."

"And I distinctly remember not listening to you."

He chuckled. "When have you ever listened to me?"

When you told me we were over. When you told me that you wanted someone with more depth than a princess who trotted around on the stage in high heels. All over again, that moment in the garage speared her heart. She could smell the motor oil again, hear the harsh tones in Jack's voice, see his back as he walked away.

"Are you still trying to be a tomboy, Meri Prescott?" Jack asked, his voice low. "Because you were always a better princess."

She looked at his face now, the tease in his eyes, and realized he still saw her as a silly girl who had tried to hang with the boys but hadn't been doing anything other than masquerading. He still saw the beauty queen, the dressed-up mannequin, produced and directed by Anna Lee Prescott.

Meri broke her gaze away and waved toward the table. "I made you guys some sandwiches and lemonade."

"Thank God. I was about ready to drop dead of starvation working with the devil's taskmaster here." Luke thumbed toward Jack, who just scowled at his brother and slid into a seat at the table. Jack reached for a sandwich and Luke smacked his hand. "Ladies first, you Neanderthal."

"I was just treating Meri like one of the guys. Just like the old days." He shot her a grin.

Like one of the guys. Like the girl who pretended to be what she wasn't. Nothing had changed in Jack's mind, nothing at all.

Meri backed up and shook her head. Her stomach started to rumble, and she pressed her hand flat against the noise. "That's okay. I already ate. I…have some work to do." Then she excused herself and headed back inside before the memories swirling in her head could gain a foothold. And before she could fall for a charming grin and a pair of sexy blue eyes that still saw her as the beauty queen she used to be—not the complicated woman she had become.

Chapter Seven

By the time they wrapped up for the day, Jack and Luke had knocked out the siding and finished repairing the front porch. He'd made a decent dent in the woodpile already this week. All that was left to do at Ray's house was pull the weeds and trim the shrubs around the house. The work he'd started so zealously a year ago had nearly come to an end.

Which left Jack at loose ends. Not a place he liked to be. Not since…

THAT DAY.

Hell, he could have quit last week, delayed the siding repairs until fall. Could have spent his day at the garage, finishing up the transmission work on Joey McCoy's Chevy. He could have stayed at his own house, working his way down the endless to-do list that came attached to a fixer-upper.

But he'd lingered at Ray's, his attention divided, hell, almost gone, every time Meri stepped outside. To him, Meri had always been a paradox—a teenager who wore a floppy hat everywhere to protect her complexion from any hint of a tan, but also one who would sneak out of the house in the middle of the night to go look at the stars. As she got older, though, the girl who would sneak out began to disappear, replaced inch by inch by someone he didn't recognize. Someone who worried about her makeup and her manicure, who was never seen without everything in perfect alignment. Like the Borg in *Star Trek*, Meri Prescott had become a walking, talking beauty queen with no patience for anything out of place.

That was what had finally driven him away from her—the realization that they were two very, very different people, and always would be.

Except maybe now. The years away, the new life she'd established, even the scar on her face had softened her somehow, erasing that perfect, porcelain doll she had once been. He liked that. A lot.

Maybe too much.

"You know, you're not half-bad at this renovation thing," Luke said as he loaded their tools into an empty bucket and hefted it into the storage shed. "Maybe you should make an honest man of yourself and start a business or something."

"I'm working for Dad right now, keeping the garage running."

"And he'll be back to running the place next week, which means you'll only be working there part-time. Besides, Dad is planning on retiring in a few years, and has made it clear that none of us has to become a second-generation garage owner. You love working outside, making things, building things. Why not do that instead?"

"Because starting a business means crap like paperwork and taxes and—"

"And that's called being a grown-up, Jack. You work, give Uncle Sam his cut—"

"Uncle Sam already took enough of me. More than enough." Jack tossed the extra siding onto the truck and stalked over to the driver's side. Before he could climb into the cab, Luke put a hand on his arm.

"Listen, I know you went through a ton of crap over there. Stuff no man should go through. Stuff you're probably going to be dealing with for years. But that doesn't mean your life ended in Afghanistan."

"What the hell do you know about what I went through?"

"I don't know anything," Luke said quietly. "But I know you and I know this…angry, lost man you've become isn't my brother. You gotta start taking some steps forward, Jack, so you're not stuck in Neutral forever. Start a business. Get some business cards. Get an appointment book and put something in it besides *be a miserable ass today.*"

"What gives you the right to tell me how to live my life?"

Luke flipped over his wrist and pointed to the vein running down his forearm. "It comes with the DNA. And speaking of those you are related to, those who still love you even when you're as pissed-off as a badger caught in a bear trap, you *are* going home to take a shower and show up at Mama's for dinner. Right?"

The way Luke said the last word brooked no room for argument. It said *either agree or I'll drag you there myself, even if you're sweaty and covered with sawdust.*

"Luke—"

"Pot roast. Mashed potatoes. And the jerks who love you." Luke grinned. "How can you resist that combination?"

Jack wanted to disagree. He wanted to retreat to his cabin and sit there until the sun sank into the lake and the moon kissed the water with silver. He wanted to sit there and have a beer or two or ten and feel good and sorry for himself. He wanted to sit there until the shadows retreated from the corners of his mind, and sweet peace returned.

Peace. It had been a long damned time since he'd had anything even close to peace in his life. And sitting on the porch, getting drunk and watching the sun go down sure as hell wasn't going to bring it back. He'd tried that—about two hundred times since he got home from the war—and it had yet to do anything but numb the pain for a few brief hours.

Maybe it would do him some good to try something. Something with at least a little nutritional value. And if the suffocating well-meaning attempt of his family to make him feel better got to be too much, there was always the porch and the case of Bud.

Hell, even the thought of sitting out there tonight, as he had too many nights already, depressed him.

"Fine, I'll go."

Luke's brows arched but he quickly covered his surprise. "Dinner's at—"

"Six. It's been at six every night for the past thirty years. I'll be there." He waved his brother away. "You don't have to wait on me. If I say I'll be there, I'll be there."

Jack got into his truck, put it into gear and drove the

short mile from Ray's cabin to his own. He laid out some clothes and hopped in the shower, knowing that if he stopped moving, or stopped to think, he'd change his mind. He tidied a house that didn't need tidying, checked the mail and wasted a few minutes reading the junk mail advertising a pool service and another piece telling him now was the perfect time to buy a new sofa. Then, when he could stand the silence and wait no longer, he got in his truck again and drove across town.

As soon as the thick trees of the lake area were in his rearview mirror, Jack began to tense. The grand mansions of the old South began to dominate the landscape, with their wide, friendly verandas and sherbet-colored siding. Once, Jack had dreamed of owning a house here. Imagined himself coming home to a wife, a couple kids, a goofy golden retriever. Then he'd gone to Afghanistan and all those dreams seemed like the stupid, silly fantasies of a kid who didn't know anything about life.

He didn't fit on these streets. He never really had. The problem was, he had no idea where he fit anymore.

He turned right, then left, then another left and down to the end of a cul-de-sac. The Barlow home sat in the center of the curve, a battered basketball hoop mounted on the garage and presiding over the driveway. Jack stopped the truck a few feet away and just stared at the house, debating. What had seemed like a good idea earlier now made him want to turn around and put the pedal to the metal.

Then he saw Meri pull into the driveway, park and step out of her Toyota. She'd swept her hair into an imperfect bun, leaving a few tendrils dancing across her cheeks. She'd changed out of shorts and a T-shirt into a pale blue sundress that skimmed her calves and hugged her figure. He waited, sure she would look over and see him, but she just shifted a big white bowl into her hands, closed the car door with one swift bump of her hip, then strode up the walkway and rang the bell. He waited a second, to see if Ray got out, too, but the older man wasn't in the car. Must have decided not to come. Jack couldn't blame him. Heck, if he hadn't been related, he wouldn't be here either.

That was a lie. He was here because he knew Meri was coming. Because as much as he thought he had put her in his past, there was something different about this Meri, something intriguing, something that hadn't been there before. Something he wanted to explore.

In the end, it was the casual yet sexy bump of her hip that had him putting his truck in gear, pulling into the drive and parking behind her aging sedan. He hopped out and hurried up the walk, coming up behind her before the door opened. "Here, Meri, let me take that bowl for you. And your car is running rough, so I can take a look at it tomorrow if you want."

Just call him Sir Galahad.

Meri turned to him, her eyes hidden by sunglasses. "Jack. You came."

"You sound disappointed."

"Surprised, that's all. I thought…well, Luke said…" She shook her head and a smile curved up her face. Meri had always had a stunning smile, the kind that filled her face with sunshine. He liked that smile. Liked it a lot. "I'm glad you're here."

He wanted to ask if she really meant that, but the door opened before he could speak, and there was a flurry of joy from his mother and her three dogs. The muddle of mutts surged forward in a burst of barking and tail wagging. Jack's mother opened her arms and drew both of them into a quick hug.

"Meri! Jack!" Della Barlow exclaimed. "Oh, my, you all are a sight for sore eyes."

"Mama, you just saw me last week."

His mother drew back and gave him a light swat. "It was three weeks ago, Jackson, and one would think you were living on the other side of the moon, considering how often you come around anymore."

"I've been busy."

"And I've been mourning all those empty chairs around my dining room table. My Lord, this house does echo without you boys around." Then she brightened. "But they won't be empty tonight. I've got two of my three boys home, and company I haven't seen in a long time, and that is good enough for me. Come on in before dinner gets cold."

Jack trailed behind his mother and Meri, who kept up a lively conversation with Della about the meal and the salad Meri had brought as the women headed down the hall and into the kitchen. Jack detoured to the parlor—though over the years the formal parlor had become more and more like a man cave than anything from a Margaret Mitchell novel. Della had tried to hold onto the space for a long time, insisting it was good for entertaining. When she realized most of the people who came to the Barlow house congregated around the food, she let her husband have his space. He'd filled it with leather reclining sofas, a big-screen TV and a coffee table that Della said looked like someone had taken a sledgehammer to the finish.

Bobby Barlow got to his feet when his son entered the room. He was a tall man, though his posture was stooping a bit with age. He still had a fit, trim body and sinewy, muscular arms from years of working on cars, repairing their engines and buffing out dents and scratches. Jack and his older brother, Mac, had worked almost every summer for their dad, starting with fetching tools. Luke had never been very good with engines, so it was the other two Barlow boys who became Bobby's right-hand men. Until Jack grew up and went in the military and Mac went off to become a too-busy-for-family CEO, as evidenced by his absence tonight. Luke must have only had time to drag one recalcitrant brother home.

This past spring, Bobby had had a knee replacement that had kept him sidelined for several weeks. Jack had stepped in. Now, looking at his father, he wondered if Luke was right that Bobby wanted to retire. Dad seemed happy here, in his recliner, without the stress of the business on his shoulders. He'd gone fishing several times this year, and had started taking walks with Della as part of his knee rehabilitation. Jack reminded himself to talk to Mac about the garage. Maybe the two of them should take it over for Dad.

You love working outside, making things, building things. Why not do that instead? You gotta start taking some steps forward, Jack, so you're not stuck in Neutral forever. Start a business. Get some business cards. Get an appointment book and put something in it besides be a miserable ass today.

Maybe Luke had a point.

"'Bout damned time you got here," Bobby said as Jack walked in the room, but his words lacked any punch.

He reached out and drew his youngest son into a quick, tight hug.

"Sorry, Dad. I was busy working on Ray's cottage."

Bobby waved that off. "I'm not mad. And anything you do for Ray is good with me. My God, that man is practically family. No, I've been waiting for you because I need someone to tell your brother he's an idiot."

Jack grinned and turned to Luke. "You're an idiot."

Luke scowled. "Just because I put a few bucks on Duke doesn't make me an idiot."

"It does when my Tar Heels are playing. Everyone knows North Carolina has the best pitcher in the country." Bobby sat back in the recliner and popped out the footrest like an exclamation point.

"Is that why they're oh and six this season so far?" Luke popped a couple nuts from the bowl on the coffee table into his mouth.

Bobby threw up his hands. "See what I got to deal with? Makes me seriously question your DNA, Luke."

Jack chuckled. "I repeat, Luke, you are an idiot. Never argue with your future inheritance."

"True. That ball cap collection should make me at least ten dollars richer on eBay."

Bobby tossed a pillow at Luke. "That's it. You're out of the will."

"Again? That makes three times this month." Luke grinned, then waved to the seat beside him on the sofa. "Have a seat, you traitor, and watch Duke make me a richer man."

Jack settled into the leather cushion. The sofa molded around him like a glove, begging him to stay longer, to make himself at home. Still, Jack remained tense, uneasy. He faked a smile and feigned interest in the game. His brother and father parried gentle digs like tennis players, but Jack mostly stayed quiet. He noticed his father glancing over at him from time to time, concern filling the spaces in his face, but Bobby didn't say anything.

Jack was on the edge of the seat, about to leave, sure he couldn't take one more minute in an environment that had once been comforting and instead had become a heavy blanket of expectations, when Meri walked into the room.

In an instant, the tension in Jack's chest eased. He drew in a deep breath and caught the faintest whisper of Meri's perfume. Cherry and almonds. Sweet and soft, all at once.

And nice. Very, very nice.

"Dinner is served," Meri said. "And Della told me to tell you that you three are invited to the table, as long as you behave like gentlemen and not cavemen."

"Your mother spoils all the fun," Bobby grumbled, but he did it with a smile. Of all the couples Jack knew, his parents were two of the happiest people he'd ever seen. Even after almost forty years of marriage, they held hands in the movies and exchanged kisses in front of their kids. Almost gave Jack hope for his own future.

Almost.

Meri took a seat on the far right side of the dining room table. Jack's parents took the seats on either end, and Luke headed for the seat next to Meri. He put a hand on the back of the chair, then shot Jack a just-kidding grin and circled over to the other side of the table. Jack scowled. Even his brother was a damned closet matchmaker. Jack settled in beside Meri and tried to quell the silly leap of joy in his chest when she shot him a quick smile.

Jack reached for the bowl of biscuits, but his mother

leaned forward and tapped him on the wrist. "Gratitude before gluttony, Jackson." Then she nodded toward her husband. "Robert."

"Why is it you only call me by my given name at dinner, Della?"

"Because a family meal is a solemn occasion." She waved toward her husband. "Grace?"

His father clasped his hands, bowed his head, and the others followed suit. "Thank you for the food on our table, the love in our hearts and the beautiful but stubborn woman I married, who keeps it all together and keeps me in line. Amen."

Della's *amen* came with a schoolgirl giggle and a slight blush. "All right, everyone, let's eat."

When Jack had arrived at his parents' house, he'd planned on eating and leaving as fast as possible. But as the conversation around the table rippled like a wake from a boat, he began to settle into the comfort of being home, in familiar surroundings, with familiar people, for the first time in the year he'd been home.

"You're going to tell me this is all healthy?" Bobby said.

"It's as healthy as I can make it." Della smiled. "And don't you tell me health food is akin to eating roadkill, Robert Barlow. I'm aiming to make sure you stay around a good long time, driving me crazy."

"So you can stuff me with cauliflower and hang me on the mantel." The words came out as a grumble, but he dished up an extra helping of the faux potatoes anyway.

"Meri, I'll be sure to fix a plate for your grandfather. It's a shame he couldn't come."

"He'd sure appreciate it, Mrs. Barlow. Grandpa really wanted to be here, but he overdid it today," Meri said. "He was tired. I told him to rest instead of coming to dinner. Though I do hope you invite him again sometime. It'd be good for him to get around other people."

"I was just telling Jack that Ray is practically family. Hell, I've known him almost as long as I've known my own name," Bobby said with an affirmative nod. "Good man, your grandfather."

"He's had a hard time since my grandma died," Meri said. "I think that's why he let his health go, which led to the heart attack. But now he seems to be coming around, and doing much better."

"I think it's because he has you there," Della said. "Ray always did have a soft spot for you, Meri."

"Losing the love of your life…" Bobby shook his head. "That's bound to send a man into a tailspin. I thank the good Lord I have my Della here with me. And I pray the three idiots I raised will come to their senses and settle down before I get too old to remember the names of my grandkids."

"Don't go getting me married off, Dad," Luke said, putting up his hands, warding off the suggestion. "I'm nowhere near ready for that."

"He has trouble committing to a brand of toothpaste," Jack muttered.

"Speak for yourself, Mr. Never Got Over—"

From under the table, Jack kicked Luke before he could finish the sentence. "Did anyone ever tell you that you talk too much?"

Luke gave his brother a bite-me grin.

"Boys, we have company, so quit acting like you left your manners rotting on the side of the road." Della gave them the evil eye, then brightened as she turned to Meri and gave her a sweet smile. "Tell me, Meri, what have you been up to in the years since you left Stone Gap?"

"A whole lot of nothing, my mama would say," Meri said with a shrug, as if the remark didn't sting, but Jack swore he saw a flicker of sadness on Meri's delicate features. "Which means I dropped out of pageants and went to work on the other side of them instead."

"The other side?" Luke asked. "If that means helping the girls change in and out of their dresses, I'm applying for that job."

His mother swatted him. "You are not too old to be sent to your room, Lucas."

"Mama, you haven't grounded me since I was fifteen," Luke said, with the winning smile that had gotten him out of detentions and dishes. "That's because I'm the charming one."

"If you're the charming one, what am I?" Jack said.

"The one we keep around to make fun of." Luke forked up a big bite of roast.

Mama rolled her eyes, and bit back a smile. "Ignore my boys. Apparently, evolution takes a little longer on the male side of the Barlow family tree. As you were saying, Meri?"

"I went into photography instead. I started doing portraits and working at pageants and dance recitals when I was in college, but found I really loved landscapes and cityscapes."

"That sounds wonderful." Della buttered a roll, then added a slab of margarine to her faux potatoes. "Now that you're back in Stone Gap, are you going to open a studio here in town?"

"Where's the barbecue sauce?" Bobby said, glancing around the white expanse of table.

"There isn't any," Della said, then turned back to Meri. "I mean, if you're staying, that is."

"I'm here for a while," Meri said, and Jack noticed how she deftly avoided the question about permanence. So how long was a while, exactly? And why did Jack care? "I'm here mostly to take care of my grandpa."

"Well, if there's one thing Stone Gap could use, it's a great photographer. This is such a beautiful part of the country. We need someone who sees it the way the rest of us do."

"No barbecue sauce?" Bobby said. He lifted the salt and pepper, peeked around the bread bowl. "How am I supposed to eat my pot roast?"

"Barbecue sauce has too much sugar, Robert. I made an au jus sauce instead."

His father scowled. "It should be called *Aw, jeez, that isn't what I wanted.*"

"I do it all for love, dear." Della gave him a big smile, and that softened the edges of Bobby's scowl.

"I didn't know you became a photographer," Jack said, turning to Meri, his dinner forgotten and growing cold on his plate. Of all the careers he would have thought Meri would have, being on the other side of a camera lens never even made the list. She'd loved taking pictures as a hobby, but he'd have bet a million dollars on Meri going into modeling or television work. "What happened to becoming Miss America?"

The room quieted, and everyone looked at Jack. Then at Meri.

She dropped her gaze to her plate and picked at the faux potatoes. "I never wanted to be Miss America. That was my mother's dream."

"Well, I think she's beautiful enough to be Miss America," Della said. "Always has been."

"Thank you, Mrs. Barlow."

"Never seemed that way before," he muttered.

Meri shifted to face him. "What are you saying, Jack?"

Damn it. He was in a foul mood—all this family togetherness and happiness had him missing the solitude of his cabin in the woods—and he was taking it out on Meri. Plus he was curious about the Meri who had returned, so different from the one who had left. The Meri he had thought would never be the kind of woman he wanted.

"Nothing."

"Would anyone like some more mashed potatoes?" Della asked, hoisting the bowl.

"Don't call them mashed potatoes," Bobby grumbled. "That's false advertising."

Della made a face at her husband. "When your cholesterol is no longer higher than the national debt, you can tell me what to call my potatoes."

"Did you think I *enjoyed* being trotted across that stage like a prize pony?" Meri said to Jack.

He shrugged. "Never saw you saying no."

What was he, some kind of sadist? Why couldn't he let it go? Why did he keep acting like an ass, and effectively driving her away, like a virus he didn't want to catch?

"Then I guess you didn't know me that well, Jack. Or maybe you didn't know me at all." She shook her head and toyed with the beef on her plate. "Or maybe this is just some new side of you coming out that I don't recognize."

"Nobody recognizes me anymore," he said, then he shoved back the chair, so fast it screeched a protest on the hardwood floor. "Especially me."

He threw his napkin down and headed out the door, out into the warm June air, out to where he could breathe and think again. Except that damned panther fashioned out of guilt and regret stalked him like easy prey.

Chapter Eight

"What the hell was that?" The words left Meri's mouth before she descended the first stair into the small yard that the Barlow house sat on. Behind the house lay acres and acres of woods, thick trees with dark leafy canopies. Home of forts and adventures and frog hunting with the boys when she'd been young, but now, with Jack standing like a sentry in front of the darkening forest, the woods seemed to carry a magical secrecy to them, as if the oaks knew something no one else did.

Jack didn't turn around. "Nothing. Just go back to dinner."

"You knew I hated those pageants. I told you a hundred thousand times how much I hated them."

"Sorry."

The single word, thrown to her like a bone at a dog, set off a spark inside of Meri. She marched down the lawn and stepped in front of Jack. He flicked a glance at her, then returned his attention to the dark, empty woods beyond them. "What is wrong with you? When did you become so…mean?"

His jaw hardened. His eyes narrowed. His shoulders tensed. For a second, she thought he was going to march off and leave her there.

"Quit pushing me, Meri. Just leave me alone."

"Is that what you really want, Jack Barlow? Because I can sure as hell walk away and leave you alone forever. Yes, you went through hell in the war, but that doesn't give you a pass to treat everyone around you like crap." She turned on her heel.

Jack reached out and grabbed her arm. "Don't go, please."

She bit her lower lip, debating. "Why?"

"Because you're right—I've been an ass. In fact, most days I perfect the art of being a jerk." He toed at the grass. "But you don't understand, I just…I don't see the world the same way I used to."

"Then tell me, Jack. Don't shut me out. We used to be friends, remember? Before everything else."

"You don't want to hear my stories. Hell, I don't even think I want to talk about them."

She thought about Grandpa's words. Of how Grandma had waited and cared and how that mix of patience and love had finally healed her grandfather's wounds. Jack deserved the same, and maybe she could help him get there.

Not because she loved him, of course, but because he was an old, dear friend. Because they had both lost someone they loved, and they both had scars the world didn't see. Nothing more.

"Talk to me, Jack. Please."

He stood there a long time, silent for so long she almost gave up. Then finally the words began to drip out of him, slow, quiet, edged with pain. "Do you know what I see when I look out there?" He pointed toward the forest.

She glanced over her shoulder. "I don't know. Trees? Squirrels?"

"I see hiding places for snipers. I see dark, ominous mounds that are concealing an IED. I see bodies under the fallen logs, danger around the corner and men waiting to kill the troops I'm supposed to protect. I see *death*, Meri. Death and danger and hell."

"Jack, it's just trees. There's—"

"Don't you understand? Nothing is just *anything* to me, not anymore. Every car backfiring is an explosion in my head. Every man who glances at me is a terrorist with a bomb strapped to his chest. I hear a plane fly overhead and I have to fight the urge to dive for cover because I'm waiting to hear the whistle of a bomb just before it hits the ground." He clenched and unclenched his fists, then shook his head. "I'm not the same anymore, and I never will be. So stop trying to re-create something that is gone. Dead."

The harsh tone sent her back a few steps. She glanced again at the woods, trying to see what he saw, trying to imagine what had happened on the other side of the world. Trying to put herself in his shoes, in the eyes and life of a man who had witnessed unspeakable tragedies in a hot desert on the other side of the world.

Then her hand fluttered to her scar, fingers sliding along that indented crescent shape, and she understood. "I can't pretend that I know what you went through over there. How many nightmares haunt your dreams, but I want to tell you that I…understand."

He scoffed. "How can you understand? How can anyone understand? I went through hell, Meri. Talking about it doesn't make it go away. All it does is bring it all back up again, like bile waiting in my gut. So quit trying to make it easier."

The harsh words were a wall, designed to push her away. But she stayed, recognizing in Jack some of the same pain that had haunted her in the months since the attack. "Okay, maybe you don't want to talk about what happened to you, and I get that. But let me talk to you about me. About what I see when I look in the woods."

She didn't wait for him to reply, she just kept going, the words escaping her in a small, tight whisper. "I see a man with a knife waiting for me to round the corner. I hear the sound of his breathing, heavy, fat, while he's waiting. But I'm too focused on getting the shot, on my job, to see him, to process what is about to happen. I see his shoes first, and they're so white against the dark night, the buildings I'm trying to frame against a waning light. I stay where I am, though, thinking he's going to keep going. But he doesn't, and then I see a flash of silver, and by the time I process it, realize it's a blade, it's too late, and I can't move, I can't scream, I can't…"

She sucked in a breath, steadied herself. "I can't do anything to stop it."

"Oh, Meri…" Jack reached for her, but she stepped back.

"I didn't tell you because I need someone to hold my hand or tell me it's all going to be okay. I know all that. I know, with time, it'll get easier and I'll be okay. That's why I'm here, to take care of my grandfather, and to take care of me." She reached for Jack's hand and held it tight with her own. "I told you because you need to know you aren't the only one afraid to look at the woods."

"I'm not afraid." He shook his head. "That's not my problem."

"Yeah, you are. You're terrified that if you let whatever is in the woods, those deep, dark woods in your head—" she cupped his cheek "—if you let all that come back into your life, you won't be able to deal with it."

Jack stayed silent.

"Do you remember what Eli used to say?"

Jack's face pinched. "Why are you bringing him up?"

"Because we both loved him, and we both miss him."

"I'm done talking about this. I'm going to get some dessert."

Jack started to turn away, but she stopped him. "Eli used to say that the only way to beat the monsters in the closet was to talk about them. He was right. Whatever demons you are holding in here—" she placed a hand on his chest, where the steady *thump-thump* of his heart beat against her palm "—are going to keep on haunting you until you talk about them."

He scowled and jerked away. "What are you, my psychiatrist? The army already gave me one of those. Didn't do me a damned bit of good. In fact, they've given me a whole truckful of psychologists since I got back. I don't need another one."

She'd been wrong. She wasn't the right one to bring Jack out of this hole. She wasn't her grandmother and he wasn't Grandpa Ray. She should just let it go and quit trying to save a cause that didn't want to be saved.

"No, Jack. I'm just your friend. Last I checked, those

didn't come by the truckful, so maybe you should stop trying to drive away the few you do have."

The worms, squirming in their dirt display and wriggling against the glass case, almost made Meri turn back. After the crickets she'd seen earlier, she wasn't so sure this was the best idea she'd ever had.

No, she was doing this. She'd told Jack to face what scared him most. It was time she did the same—even if her fears were only a few inches long and squirming in some dirt.

"I'll take a dozen," she said to Big Joe, a hearty beer-barreled man who fit his name. He'd owned Big Joe's Tackle and Bait for as long as anyone in Stone Gap could remember.

He thumbed at his suspenders and considered the squirmers in the refrigerated case. "You planning on doing some serious fishing, you might want to get two dozen."

Serious fishing? She hadn't done any fishing. Ever. But serious sounded like a good plan, so she nodded and said, "Two dozen it is."

He scooped the worms into a white paper container, then poked some holes into a lid and slapped it on top before handing it to Meri. She swore she could feel the worms squirming against the sides, trying to get out. *Ew.*

"You Anna Lee Prescott's daughter?" Big Joe asked. "The one that used to do all those beauty pageants?"

"Yes." The scar arcing across her face seemed to burn, like a scarlet letter announcing that she was no longer a beauty queen. "But I don't do pageants anymore."

"I can't blame you. Ain't nothing I hate more than getting gussied up. My wife's lucky I change my shirt for

Sunday church." He chuckled. "I gotta say, I never took you for the fishing type."

"I'm not. Or, I haven't been. But I plan on being the fishing type now." She held up the container of worms and tried not to be grossed out by the soft sound of them wriggling along the inside of the paper walls.

When she'd been a young girl, she'd tried to be like everyone else—tried to be a tomboy who climbed trees and played in mud. She'd skinned a few knees, scraped a few elbows, but as she got older, she'd realized she had to make a choice: either take the pageants seriously or defy her mother outright and go off on her own path. Meri had caved to the pageant world, and her momentary brush with adventures had stopped. She'd focused on keeping every inch of her body perfect, show ready.

Now she was hungry, as if she'd walked into an all-you-can-eat restaurant. She wanted every one of those things she had denied herself for so long, all those activities she had watched her friends do years ago. She might be a little late to the party, but that wasn't going to stop her now.

"Yup, I'm definitely going to be the fishing type now."

"Then you're gonna need a few supplies," Big Joe said.

By the time Meri left, she had a new fishing reel, a small tackle box with a few tools, a khaki-colored vest to hold what, she wasn't quite sure, and a thick book that was akin to *Fishing for Dummies*. She set the container of worms on the passenger seat and kept glancing at it on the short ride back to Grandpa Ray's, sure that the worms were going to crawl out at any moment. But nothing earthly escaped. Thank God.

"Grandpa, I've got the bait," she called as she entered the dim cottage. "Are you ready to go?"

Grandpa waved to her from his recliner in the living room. An old black-and-white war movie played on the television in front of him. "Oh, Merry Girl, I'm sorry to say I'm not feeling so well, after all. I'm fixing to take a nap."

She crossed to him and put a hand on his forehead. His skin was cool, his color a little pale. "Are you okay?"

"Just worn out from a busy few days. Nothing a little sleep won't cure."

"We can go fishing another day. No problem."

"What, and let some perfectly good worms go to waste? No, no, you go fishing."

"By myself?" She laughed. "I have no idea how to bait a hook or cast a line or anything else. With my luck, I'll probably end up hooking my own thumb."

"Then ask Jack to go along. He's been working too hard as it is. He's been out in the heat all day, working on that cranky lawn mower of mine. He needs a break."

Ask Jack? After the way things had ended on Sunday night at his mother's house, she didn't think that was a good idea. She'd left immediately after their argument in the yard, skipping out on the apple crumble, after all.

Then she thought of that kiss the other day—that OMG-amazing kiss—that had seemed to say Jack was interested in her, wasn't trying to push her away. For heaven's sake, she was getting so many mixed messages from the man, maybe she should just avoid him altogether.

She'd tried going out with her camera this morning and never even took the Nikon out of the bag. Hence the fishing, which at least got her out into the nature she loved but didn't force her to move past that wall that hit her every time she looked at the camera bag.

"Jack won't go fishing with me," Meri said. "We… haven't exactly been getting along lately."

Grandpa Ray considered that. "Then I guess you're going to have to bring out the big guns. Tell him I'll let him take my brand-new ultralight spinning rig. He's been eyeing that thing ever since I bought it, and ever since I caught a nice twenty-pound largemouth bass with it. Fisherman envy will get Jack out on the boat, guaranteed. That, and I bet he'd be willing to bait those hooks for you, too, unless you're fixin' to put those squirming suckers on the hook yourself."

She didn't think any kind of fishing pole was going to change Jack's mind, but the thought of going alone on her very first fishing trip didn't sound like fun. Nor did the thought of baiting the hooks. She'd apparently forgotten that very important step when she'd bought live bait. Should have gone with the fake worms instead.

She considered forgetting the fishing altogether, then decided she only had so much time in Stone Gap, and she wanted to make use of every moment she could—doing all the things she had avoided for too long, because they weren't ladylike or would risk her getting a cut or sunburn or something else horrifying to her mother.

"I know he's a bear," Grandpa said, "but if you give Jack a chance…"

"I've already given him thirty chances."

"Well, maybe he needs thirty-one. He's a man, after all, and sometimes our kind is too stubborn for our own good."

"You have a point." She pressed a kiss to her grandfather's cheek. "Thanks, Grandpa."

She gathered up the pile of supplies she'd bought at Big Joe's, slid on the vest, then headed outside and toward the lake. Jack was just coming out of the shed, wiping his hands on a rag. He saw her—and started to laugh.

"What the hell are you doing?"

"Going fishing."

He cast a glance over her attire, then at the pole in her hands and the container of bait dangling from two fingers. "Let me guess. Big Joe told you that you should have all this crap?"

"Well…yeah."

"You know what you need to go fishing?" Jack stuffed the rag into his back pocket, then took two steps closer to her. "A line, some bait and a hell of a lot of patience. You've got two out of three."

She glanced down at the gear in her hands. "I thought I bought everything I needed at Joe's."

"You did." He took another step closer and her pulse accelerated. "You're just missing the patience part."

She waved him off. "I'm patient."

At that, Jack laughed. Heartily. "You? You're the one Merriam-Webster uses as the poster child for *im*patient."

"Maybe I was that way when I was younger, but not anymore." This time, she was the one who moved into his space, raising her chin to his. "And I can prove it to you."

"Oh, yeah? Prove it? How?"

The way he said the words, dark and low, sent a tremor through Meri. Who was she kidding? She'd never gotten over him. Every time she was around him, she was a teenager again, with her heart flippity-flopping in her chest and her breath getting caught in her throat. She was kidding herself if she thought this was just about baiting a hook or getting Jack out of a bad mood. This was about Jack Barlow and her, and unfinished business.

"Go fishing with me," she said. "And I'll show you how patient I can be."

"Go fishing. With you. Today."

She nodded. "Put down those tools. Put away that to-do list, and just float around the lake with me for the rest of the afternoon. Whoever catches the most fish wins."

A smile curved up one side of his face. "Wins what?"

She thought about it for a second. "How about lunch?"

"I already ate. And besides, a grilled cheese sandwich or a turkey club isn't exactly high stakes, wouldn't you agree?"

"Is that what this is going to be? High-stakes fishing?"

His gaze swept over her, those blue eyes filled with a tease and a temptation. "If you're going to challenge me with something, Meri Prescott, be prepared to take it all the way."

Heat coiled in her belly, flushed on her chest. "And, uh, how far do you want to take this?"

He gave her a lopsided grin. "Loser dives into the lake—"

"I can handle that."

"Naked."

A heartbeat passed between them. She swallowed hard. "Naked?"

His grin widened. "Hasn't Miss America ever gone skinny-dipping?"

"Don't call me that. I was never Miss America. And no, I've never gone skinny-dipping. Either way, I don't plan on doing that." At least not with him. Because getting naked in front of Jack Barlow would be far too tempting.

He took the rod from her and leaned in to whisper in her ear, sending a shiver of temptation all the way to her toes. "Then I suggest you catch one hell of a big fish."

Chapter Nine

He really needed to start thinking before he opened his mouth. In the military, Jack had never made a move without calculating the odds and weighing the risks and rewards. On tour, his mind was a constant whir of assessment of the buildings, people and routes around him. The mantle of leadership had sat heavy on his shoulders, coloring every thought, every choice.

But when Meri stood in front of him, with that lilt in her smile and that sparkle in her eyes, all coherent thought went out the window. His wants and needs became very simple. *Make her smile more. Hear her laugh.* And most of all, *find a way to make her stay.*

He was clearly a masochist. Because every time he saw Meri, he thought of Eli, and when he thought of Eli—

Jack wanted to crawl into a dark, cold cave. The guilt, the regret, piled on his chest until he felt as if he was swimming through a thick soup, trying to find his way to the surface before the weight of the water dragged him down again.

Then Meri would smile at him and it was like the sun parting the clouds. The darkness would ebb, the panther would step into the shadows and he had a peek again at the life he could have. If only.

"Okay, how do we do this again?" Meri stood on the dock, looking unsure and nervous, still wearing that ridiculous vest. It was kinda cute, he thought, and only accented the cleavage beneath her tank top and the long peachy length of her legs under her denim shorts.

"You just step off and into the boat. I'll keep it steady." From his seat at the stern of the skiff, he gripped the edge of the dock, then nodded toward her. "Trust me, Meri."

Trust me. Such a loaded statement. For a second, he wanted to tell her not to trust him, that he wasn't a man anyone should rely on. But then he reminded himself it was just fishing. A couple hours puttering around the lake in a boat. Nothing more.

She placed a tentative foot on the bottom of the skiff, lifted her other foot, then let out a little squeal when the boat rocked. He reached his free hand up to catch hers. She gripped him tight, then regained her balance and lowered her body to the bench seat. "That's harder than it looks."

"Harder than pirouetting around a stage in five-inch heels?"

"You liked those heels quite a lot, if I remember right."

Holy hell, yes, he'd liked those heels she wore when they'd been teenagers. Meri had been the only girl he knew in Stone Gap who wore sky-high heels that made her long legs look five miles longer and accented every inch of her curves. Too bad heels weren't appropriate footwear for fishing.

He pushed off from the dock, then pulled the cord on the outboard motor and slowly guided the skiff from the shore to the center of the lake. "I liked those heels only because they made you as tall as me."

Liar.

"And here I thought it was because you liked how they made my legs look in a bathing suit."

He grinned. "That was just a bonus."

She splashed water at him. He tried to dodge the spray, and ended up rocking the boat dangerously close to tipping into the lake, which had her squealing again and splashing him a second time. Jack laughed.

The laugh felt good. Really good. Maybe going on this fishing trip wasn't such a bad idea, after all.

Wispy clouds muted the sun's rays and drifted lazy trails across the sky. The water glistened, darkening as the boat motored toward the murky, deep center of Stone Gap Lake. It being a weekday, the lake was relatively quiet, with only a few other boats dotting the vast blue surface. A heron flew overhead, its long gangly body settling into gracefulness when it landed on the far bank.

"It's beautiful out here." Meri leaned back on the bench and turned her face to greet the sun. "So peaceful."

Peace. It wasn't something Jack knew or, hell, remembered. But out here with Meri, in the quiet murky blue of the lake, he began to wonder if perhaps he could find peace again. It seemed to linger at the fringes of his mind, just out of grasp. Maybe if he tried harder, reached farther, he'd snatch a few minutes of it here, with her.

Jack turned off the motor and grabbed one of the rods. "So are we gonna fish?"

"Do we have to?" She grinned at him. "I could just work on my tan."

"Go right ahead. It'll look great on your naked butt when you dive overboard into the lake." Jack picked a worm out of the bait container, slid it on the hook, then dropped the line over the side of the boat.

"Wait. I have to do *that* with the worm?"

He nodded. "It's not hard, just a little gross. It's best to thread it through the hook a couple times. You can't just hang it over the hook and hope for the best."

"*Thread* it through?" She blanched, then seemed to find some well of resolve inside herself. "Right. Okay. Give me a rod and the bait."

Jack did as she asked, then sat back to watch her. He thought for sure that Meri would girl out and hand him the worm and hook, but instead she surprised him, by baiting her own hook just as he had, then dropping the line on the other side of the boat from his. "I am impressed."

"It wasn't exactly hard to do. Just gross, like you said. Honestly, I didn't think I could do it." She gave him a sheepish smile. "I asked you to come along partly to bait the hook if I wimped out."

Jack chuckled. "I haven't met too many women who bait their own hook. Scratch that. The women I know who do bait their own hooks and take their own fish off the line also chew tobacco and drink moonshine."

She laughed. "You do not seriously know any women who are like that, do you?"

"Hey, this is Stone Gap. Pickin's are slim."

That made her laugh even more, and that, Jack decided, was a good thing. For the first time in a long damned time, being around the sound of laughter didn't give him that anxious feeling, as though he was in a crowd he didn't belong to.

"So, what possessed you to buy a can of worms and go fishing today?"

"I'm on a mission to do all the things I missed out on when I was doing pageants. I've been trying to make up for lost time ever since I left Stone Gap. Now I want to go fishing, camping—"

"Skinny-dipping?"

She laughed. "Sorry, Jack, that didn't make the list."

"Then you better catch more fish than I do. Don't forget our bet."

She pshawed. "Easy peasy." She shifted the rod in her hands. "Okay, so now what do I do?"

"You wait."

"How long?"

He chuckled. "You really have never fished before?"

"Do you know what kind of coronary my mother would have had if I came home smelling of bait or with a cut on my hand from some wayward hook? No, never fishing. The closest I ever got was swimming in the lake whenever I could sneak off to Grandpa Ray's."

"And whenever you tagged along with us and caught crawdads in the creek." He'd been twelve, Meri had been nine, almost ten. She'd sneaked out of the house, still wearing her pink-and-white church dress and little white shoes so shiny they reflected the sun like spotlights. Meri had clambered down the root-riddled path with Eli and Jack, her hair tangling with leaves and errant branches. She'd shied away from actually getting in the water, letting the boys do all the crawdad catching. Jack had dropped one into her palm, expecting her to scream and run away, but instead she'd beamed up at him as if he'd given her a pot of gold.

"That was a great day," Meri said. "Even if I got grounded for a month."

"A *month*?"

She shrugged, as if it was no big deal, but to Jack, it seemed a pretty severe punishment for ruining a Sunday dress. "You didn't notice I was gone that long?"

"I was twelve. I didn't notice girls at all back then. It wasn't until I was older that I noticed when you were gone."

"You did?"

A simple two-word question. He could be flip and toss back some kind of sarcastic retort, then get back to the fishing. But something about the day and the sunshine and the peace of it had wedged an opening in the shell Jack had kept around himself for the past year. "Yeah, I did. A lot."

She jiggled the line and kept her gaze on the water. "You never wrote after you went off to the military."

"I thought it was better that way." Especially after his first tour. He'd been sending letters home before that, looking forward to the letters back, but after a while he ran out of things to say. Ways to pretend that Afghanistan wasn't a hellhole and a half.

"I thought you forgot all about me." She said *me* with a lilt of a tease at the end, but the sentence held an edge of truth and hurt.

He couldn't blame her. Their breakup had been swift and unexpected. He could still see Meri standing there in his father's garage, staring at him, shocked, hurt, not understanding why he had ended their relationship the day before he shipped out. At the time, he didn't have the words to make her understand.

"I didn't forget about you, Meri," Jack said.

Their gazes met and a heartbeat passed between them, then another. "I didn't forget about you either, Jack. I wondered about you a thousand times. How you were doing, if you were back home. Eli said he was with you for a while—"

"You talked to Eli?"

"I wrote to him while he was overseas. You know Eli, though. He was never very good at keeping in touch. He'd send me an email once in a while, a letter one time, and that was about it. I wrote to him all the time, though."

"I know."

As soon as Jack said the words, he wished he had kept his mouth shut. But in his mind, he had seen the pale blue stationery in Eli's hands, and felt that odd curdle of envy all over again. Every time he'd seen Eli with one of Meri's letters, it made him think of North Carolina's glorious skies, the way the blue seemed to stretch forever. He thought of the summer he'd dated Meri, before he'd shipped off to boot camp, and the time they had lain on the float in the lake and watched delicate clouds take a languid march across the sun. In his mind, those were the years when everything was perfect and simple, and when he saw Meri's letters to Eli, he'd had a bone-deep ache for that simplicity.

"I'm glad Eli was with you," Meri said. "He told me once how scared he was and that when he got transferred to your unit, he was glad to have someone he knew and trusted there. Made him feel safer. Thank you for that, Jack. I know it made it easier on him."

Eli hadn't been safe at all, Jack wanted to scream. Not

safe for a second. Eli, that trusting, happy-go-lucky fool who had made everyone in the truck laugh five seconds before the light exploded in front of them. The light first, then the boom, then...

Jack was stuck in the middle of the damned lake. No easy escape. No back door. No way to avoid the memories, the pain, those questions in Meri's eyes. Damn it. He should have known, should have seen the situation before he'd climbed into this stupid boat.

"Were you and Eli still together when he—" her eyes filled and Jack wanted to stab himself in the heart "—when he died?"

Goddamn. Why did Meri have to be the one to ask that question? If there was anyone in the world who'd loved Eli as much as Jack, it was Meri. Eli had been Jack's best friend, but to Meri, her cousin had been the closest thing to a brother.

"I..." The truth shredded his heart and chest, took away his breath. He worked his mouth, but no more sounds came out.

I killed him, Meri.

She sat across from him, with that trusting, inquisitive look in her eyes. The same look that had been in Eli's eyes the day he walked into Jack's camp and realized Jack would be his commanding officer.

I killed him, Meri.

Jack tried again but the words lodged hard in his gut, a lead weight that Jack was sure was heavy enough to bring him and the boat and Meri to the bottom of Stone Gap Lake. How could he tell her? How could he possibly speak those words?

"Meri, I—"

"Oh! I got a bite!" She turned to the rod and started reeling in the line. "I got one!"

Jack shifted gears, grateful as hell for the fish that had chosen that moment to take the bait. He forced the memories to the back of his mind and focused on the fishing line, on the reel, on the excitement in Meri's face. "Slow and easy," he told her. "Don't rush it. You don't want to pull the hook out of his mouth." She flicked a questioning glance at him. "Yup, that's it. You got it, Meri."

The reel clicked as the line rolled back onto the brass barrel. Tension tightened the line, bowed the rod, heightened the air. But then a second later, the bend in the rod gave way and it sprang up again. "Damn," Meri said. "I think I lost him."

"That's okay. It happens. Where there's one there's always another."

"Plenty of fish in the sea, huh?"

He pulled her line into the boat and slid another worm onto the hook. Focusing on the fishing brought him back to the edge of peace again.

Once Meri's line was set, he checked his own. His worm was looking a little worse for wear, but was still tethered to the hook, so he dropped it back into the water. "Speaking of fish in the sea, how come you never got married?"

She swung her rod over to the other side of the boat and released the gossamer line, watching the silver hook disappear into the dark depths of the lake. "I could say because I haven't met Mr. Right, but that's not really it. I guess it's because I spent enough years of my life fulfilling someone else's expectations. I didn't need a ring on my finger to sentence me to more of that."

"Not all marriages are like that."

She arched a brow. "I don't see a ring on your finger, Mr. Expert."

He jiggled his rod, avoiding her gaze. "I just haven't met the right woman."

"You mean one who will put up with your faults."

"I don't have any faults." He grinned. "Just ask my mother. She thinks I'm perfect."

"She is hopelessly biased. You, my friend, have a very long list of faults." She rested her pole against the side of her leg and began ticking them off on her fingers. "You have terrible taste in music—"

"Lots of people happen to think AC/DC is a great band."

"You have matching issues."

"Matching issues?"

"Sweetheart, I hate to tell you, but camo doesn't go with red."

The *sweetheart* made his pulse skip. The boat seemed small, tight, intimate. He leaned toward her, making the boat rock a bit and their bodies wave toward each other for a second. "Honey, I hate to tell you, but everything goes with camo. That's why it's short for *camouflage*."

"So now you're a fashion expert?"

He laughed. "That is entirely your department. I'm just an expert in good ol' Southern boy apparel."

"Well, you do have that Southern boy thing down pat." She gave him a coy, flirty look.

"How's that?"

"You have that drawl when you say *honey*." She shivered and Jack wondered if his words had made her do that. "Not to mention, you have that way of looking at a woman that…"

"That what?" he asked. *"Honey?"*

Her chest rose and fell. Her green eyes darkened. "That way of looking at a woman that…makes her feel like she's the only woman in the world."

"And do you?"

"Do I what?"

"Feel like the only woman in the world?"

He wanted to know—no, needed to know. Did she want him as much as he wanted her? Did that kiss they'd shared—so hot, so short—haunt her dreams, leave her tossing and turning at night?

Jack's pole, forgotten on the bottom of the boat, gave a jerk. Meri waved toward it. "You've, uh, got one on your line, Jack."

For a second, he thought she meant he'd hooked her, but then the reel skittered across the metal bottom of the boat and the intelligence light went on in his brain. Oh, duh. A fish. The whole reason they were here today.

He gave a quick jerk, setting the hook in the fish's mouth, then reeled it in, slow and steady. A minute later, a nice five-pound bass flopped around on the floor. "That's one for me. And, uh…absolutely zero for you." He grinned. "You know what that means, don't you?"

From far off, the rumble of thunder announced an incoming summer storm. The clouds began to darken and crowd the sky, blotting out the sun. The wind shifted from a soft breeze to a strong, angry gust. "I remember our bet, Jack," Meri said. "But there's a storm coming in. We should get back."

"You're not chickening out, are you?"

"Of course not." She raised her chin a notch. "You think I'm afraid to let you see me naked?"

"I sure hope not." In those short shorts and that damnable vest, she looked silly and sexy all at the same time.

He imagined her shedding the fishing vest, shimmying out of the shorts, then standing to tug the tank top over her head. "Are you afraid to get naked with…uh, in front of me?"

"Certainly not. I'm just worried about poor Bert here."

"Bert?"

"The fish."

It took him a second to remember the bass on the floor of the boat. "You named the fish? First rule of fishing, Meri—don't name dinner." He propped the pole against the side of his seat and reached for the hook.

"Oh, don't cook him, Jack. Let him go back to his family. They're probably worried about him."

Jack didn't bother to explain that fish had about as many brain cells as worms, and he doubted any of the fish in Stone Gap Lake were worried about the fate of this one small bass. At his feet, the fish was beginning to panic, flopping faster now, its gills working furiously to find water and oxygen. The bass's eyes were wide and glassy, watching him. But instead of the fish, Jack saw Eli's eyes, filling with panic and the certain knowledge that death's long dark arm was reaching for him.

Jack sat on the hard metal bench in the skiff, immobile. His mind was back in the dusty landscape of Afghanistan, surrounded by thick smoke and twisted metal and panicked screams. *Eli, I'm sorry. I'm so damned sorry.*

"He's scared, Jack." Meri's voice, seeming to come from a thousand miles away. "Let him go. Quick, before he dies."

Get it together, soldier. Do something, damn it.

"Jack? Did you hear me? Seriously, I feel bad now. I know it's just a fish, but can we please not cook him?"

Just a fish. One of thousands in this lake, one of dozens he had caught over the years. It wasn't Eli. Was. Not. Eli.

Jack closed his eyes. Opened them again. The bass's tail flopped again, then slowed, as if the fish was giving up, giving in to the oxygen-deprived end.

"Come on, buddy," Jack said, working the hook out of the bass's mouth before reaching under the fish to scoop him up. Jack tipped his palms toward the lake and the bass slid down and into the water.

The fish lay still for a moment, and Jack's heart clutched. Too late, he'd been too late.

Then there was a flicker, a hard right with the tail and the fish was gone in a glimmer of blue-green that shimmered for a moment on the surface, then darted deep into the dark water below.

Meri reached for Jack's hand. "You're a fish hero, Jack Barlow."

"I'm not any kind of hero at all," he said, then he turned to the engine, started the motor and headed for shore. Before the storm in the air, and the one in his heart, came roaring in to ruin the day.

Chapter Ten

The shiny black Cadillac swung into Ray's driveway with a low purr. The engine shut off, then Anna Lee emerged from the air-conditioned leather interior, wearing her Sunday best on a Wednesday and the usual scowl that accompanied any detour from the genteel side of town.

Clearly, this was the first sign of the apocalypse—her mother had come to visit. Meri sighed, put down her coffee cup, then pushed through the screen door of the guest cottage and out onto the porch. "Momma. What are you doing here?"

Anna Lee swatted at the air, frowning at the cloud of gnats swarming around her hundred-dollar-an-ounce perfume. "I raised you with enough manners to answer when your mother calls you."

Her mother had tried twice to reach Meri, but she'd let

the calls go to voice mail. Maybe it was cowardly, but she just didn't want to deal with Momma's criticisms right now. "I've been busy."

Anna Lee's lips pursed. "Well, now you've made me drive all the way over here just to talk to you."

"It's not like you had to go to the other side of the moon, Momma." Though, given the number of times her mother had ventured to this side of town, it might as well have been in another solar system. "Grandpa Ray was Daddy's father, and it'd be nice if you visited him once in a while. Check on him."

Anna Lee fanned at her face. "Can we go inside? Out of the bugs and this heat?"

Meri nodded, then led the way into the guest cottage. Grandpa Ray was napping, and Meri doubted he wanted to be woken by a visit from his daughter-in-law.

Jack hadn't been around since the fishing trip yesterday. As the storm raged outside last night, Meri had tried to concentrate on playing gin rummy with Grandpa Ray, but her mind kept straying to Jack. To what he was hiding.

Every time she brought up Eli or the war, Jack threw up a wall. Maybe he was keeping something from her, or maybe he was just doing his level best not to rekindle anything with her.

If that was so, then why had he kissed her? Dared her to go skinny-dipping? And why couldn't she—who kept saying she wasn't interested in him—seem to put Jack from her mind for more than ten seconds?

"Meredith Lee, please be a hostess and provide your mother with a beverage. This infernal heat has me positively parched."

Meri led the way into the kitchen, ignoring her mother's sigh of disdain at the small, rustic quarters, then poured two glasses of lemonade. She handed one to Anna Lee, then sat across from her mother at the tiny kitchen table. Whatever had brought Anna Lee out here had to be important, but Meri defaulted to small talk instead of asking her straight out. "How is the gazebo coming along?"

"Done, and not a moment too soon. I had to get the workmen to start on the kitchen."

"You're redoing the kitchen? Again?"

"I *entertain*, Meredith. That requires constant upkeep and refreshment of my home."

It took some doing, but Meri managed to stop herself from rolling her eyes. "I think I have some gingersnaps, if you'd like something to eat."

Anna Lee waved that suggestion away and made a disapproving face that said she'd expected a daughter of hers to offer better than store-bought cookies. "I am not staying long enough to dine. I merely wanted to ask you to a party at the house."

Meri sighed. So this was the big thing that had dragged Anna Lee down to the lake. "Momma, I don't want to go to some stuffy party with people I barely know. I'm happier here, out by the lake, with the birds and the fish and yes, even the bugs."

Anna Lee pursed her lips again. "It would serve you well to make some new connections, and restore old connections."

"For what?"

"For finding employment, of course. I don't see you getting married anytime soon—" another frown for that one "—so you need to have viable employment. I know a good number of—"

"I have a job, back in New York. One that I'm returning to." *As soon as I can get myself to pick up my camera again. As soon as I stop seeing that night through the lens.*

She was the one who kept telling Jack to move on, when she needed to do the same herself. Starting with establishing a better perimeter between herself and her mother.

"I'm sure you could find better employment here, among old friends."

"I told you, I have a job."

Her mother sighed. "And what job would that be? Because I have never heard you speak about a career or any viable means of employment, Meredith Lee."

"Because you never asked, Mother."

Silence filled the space between them, seemed to ice the lemonade still in their glasses. Outside, there was the far-off sound of a chain saw, and the constant chatter of birds.

"What do you do, Meri?" her mother asked, the nickname a clear peace offering.

"I'm a photographer," Meri said. "A really good one. I even had my own exhibit at a gallery in SoHo. A travel magazine bought several of my photos of the city, and they offered me a job, starting next month."

"Meredith, taking pictures is not a career. It's a hobby. You had a career all lined up years ago and—" Anna Lee waved her hand "—then you just flushed it away."

Meri jerked to her feet. The chair screeched in protest. "Career? I never wanted to be a model. That was something *you* chose for me. Just like you chose all those pageants and dresses and hairstyles and every single thing I said and did from the day I was born. For once, I wish you would realize that I am a person with ambitions and dreams of my own, not some mannequin you dress up and parade around."

Her mother reached for her glass, calmly picked it up and sipped at the lemonade. Then she set the glass back on the table and folded her hands in her lap. "Are you serious about this photography thing?"

Meri swallowed a sarcastic retort. "Yes. Very."

"Then I would like to ask you to come to the party this coming weekend—" her mother put up a finger to head off Meri's objections "—and photograph it. It's a fund-raiser for a local charity for young girls, and perhaps we can use your pictures for post-event publicity."

Was her mother finally seeing her as something other than a dress-up doll? Finally taking her daughter's wants and needs into consideration? If so, Meri would be a fool to dismiss this olive branch. She sat back down. "I can do that."

"That would be wonderful." Anna Lee rose and gave her daughter a smile. "I'm looking forward to it."

"Me, too," Meri said. Maybe this was the beginning of a change in her relationship with her mother. Meri hoped so.

She walked Anna Lee out the door and onto the porch. Her mother turned and gave her a small hug. "And please, Meredith, be sure to dress appropriately," Anna Lee whispered in her ear. "These are very important people and I won't have you showing up...disheveled."

"I've been dressing the way you wanted me to all my life, Momma." Meri gave her a tight smile. "Why would I stop now?"

Jack paused on the path and saw the shiny black Cadillac back out of Ray's driveway. Meri stood on the porch of the guest cottage, watching the car leave, her arms wrapped around herself.

He told himself not to get involved. Not to get close to her. Because when he did, it only brought the specter of Eli into the picture. But his feet didn't listen to his brain and before he knew it, he was emerging from the grassy path that finished off the wooded trail that led from his house to Ray's.

"You okay?" he asked.

She started. "You scared me."

"Sorry. I thought you'd hear me tromping through the woods."

"You? You're quiet as a mouse. Must be all that military training."

"Yeah." He looked away as he said it. The last thing he wanted to do was talk about the military or what it had trained him—and not trained him—to do. "You okay?" he asked again.

"I tell myself that I won't let her upset me, but every time…" Meri shook her head and swiped at her eyes. "Every time she does. Damn it. I'm a grown-up. I shouldn't care what my mother thinks."

"All kids care about that. I think it comes with the birth certificate."

She gave him a watery smile. "I know, but I still wish it didn't upset me. I just keep hoping she'll change. Clearly, that's not a word in my mother's vocabulary."

He'd met Meri's mother more than once. A stern, disapproving woman who rarely smiled and had nothing but lectures for her only child. His own home had been warm and rough-and-tumble, with three boys born within four years of each other. He couldn't imagine growing up under Anna Lee's thumb.

"It is in yours."

She gave him a sad smile. "Only because I gave up. Do you know why I suddenly got on the pageant wagon with my mother? I fought it for so many years, then when I got to be a teenager, I decided to go with it, to try my hardest and maybe then, I thought, if I won this title, or that title, my mother would finally see me, and realize that I was more than just a contestant. She'd quit trying to parade me around, and she'd want to spend time with me, in someplace that didn't have a stage and a panel of judges. But in the end, it didn't matter if I won every title in the country. She didn't want a daughter. She only wanted a blue ribbon winner. Like the horses in her stable."

"She's the one who's losing out, Meri."

Meri let out a gust and waved at the empty driveway. "Tell her that."

He closed the gap between them and settled his hands on her hips. "I only need to tell one person."

"Who's that?"

"You." He cupped her chin. "You are amazing, Meredith Prescott."

She dipped her head and looked away. "I'm nothing out of the ordinary."

"You are more than out of the ordinary. You always have been."

She paused, the words taking their time settling into her mind. "Thank you, Jack. You always know how to make me smile."

The moment extended between them, forging a bond, a tether. Every time he tried to distance himself, he ended up getting closer to her. He needed to shift this from a tender moment to something else, something with distance. He let her go and took a step back. "You should probably do something this afternoon, something that will make you forget all about your mother's visit."

"Something like what?"

"Tell me something else on that list of yours. Remember? That list of things you wish you did when you were young and never did."

The tension eased in her face, her shoulders. "Well… we already went fishing. The ground's still too wet for camping. Um…" She thought a second, a finger on her lip, which had him wanting to grab that finger and kiss those lips. "Okay, this is going to sound silly."

"I promise not to laugh." He held up three fingers on his right hand. "Scout's honor."

"When were you a Boy Scout?"

"From ages seven to nine. Then Luke got us kicked out for eating all the popcorn we were supposed to sell for a fund-raiser."

Meri laughed. "That's something I could see Luke doing."

The unspoken message—Jack wasn't the fun one, Luke was. Jack had always been serious, single-minded. It had served him well in the military on missions, but in real life…not so much. "So tell me your silly idea."

She hesitated. "Okay, but remember, you promised not to laugh."

He held up the three fingers again. "Solemn word."

"I want to get one of every dessert from my aunt Betty's bakery and have a giant gorgefest picnic."

He remembered seeing her with that cupcake a couple weeks ago. She'd looked as if she was in heaven. It had been a sweet—no pun intended—window into what made Meri happy. "Every single one?"

She nodded. "Every single one. Do you know how

many times I fantasized about eating my fill of cookies and cupcakes when I'd do a pageant? How much I wanted to just run out of those ballrooms and dive headfirst into the first donut shop I saw? Plus—" she took a step closer to him and pointed a finger at his chest "—I missed the apple crumble at your mother's house the other night. I *need* my dessert."

"Are you saying that you fantasize about desserts?"

The wind between them shifted, and the resolve he'd felt a second ago to not get involved, to stay platonic, dissolved. He thought of that kiss they'd shared—that one amazing kiss—and how much he wanted another, and another after that. A little teasing, a little flirting... it couldn't hurt. Could it?

"Well, not *just* desserts." A sexy smile curved up one side of her face, and he wondered if she had felt the same shift, if she was thinking about that kiss as much as he was. "There are other decadent things I fantasize about having...and doing."

A fire roared to life in his gut. It took everything he had to keep himself from dragging her off to the nearest flat surface after the way she said *decadent*. "Decadent like...what?"

"Hmm...I might need a cupcake to answer that question."

He shifted closer to her, his gaze on her lips. "Has anyone ever told you that you're a tease?"

"I'm a woman in need of sugar," she said, then gave him a flirty pout. "I'm not above using my feminine wiles for a little chocolate."

"How about I, uh, run into town and bring back the desserts? You get the picnic together." Hell, about now he'd run to Jupiter and Mars for what she wanted.

"You'd really do that for me?"

For the way she was looking at him right now, he'd fly to the moon and back. "It won't take long. Just keep thinking chocolate—"

She closed her eyes and bit her lower lip. "Mmm..."

God help him. "Cake."

Meri licked her lips and he bit back a groan.

"Whipped cream." He drew out the last two words, then trailed a finger along her lower lip. She opened her mouth against his finger. His groin ached. He exhaled a long, shuddering breath. "Extra whipped cream."

"You're feeding my fantasies, Jack Barlow." Dark desire filled her eyes, and the world seemed to close to just them. It had always been like this—he and Meri treading on the edge of something undeniable.

He thought of all the fantasies he'd had about her in the last couple of weeks. The nights he had lain awake, knowing she was only a mile away, probably sleeping in something skimpy with the window open and the breeze off the lake washing over her skin. How he'd pictured sliding into her, dipping his head to take one of her nipples in his mouth while she arched against him and he drove them both over the edge. "That's my goal, Meri Prescott."

"I'll be waiting, then." She pressed a kiss to his finger, then stepped back.

Jack dashed back to his truck, excited as if he was sixteen again and about to go on his first date, and roared down the road to town. By the time he reached Betty's Bakery, his heartbeat had slowed and reality set in. He'd volunteered for this trip—alone.

For months, he'd been driving by the bakery, always with the intent of stopping in, of going up to Betty and

George and explaining what had happened. The closest he'd come was the day Meri was there, and he'd finally walked through the door. But in the end, he'd left without saying what he needed to say.

The hand-painted sign in the window was still turned to Open. No other cars were parked in the angled spaces outside the shop. Jack parked the truck and sat there, the keys in his hands.

Eli used to say that the only way to beat the monsters in the closet was to talk about them, Meri had said. *Whatever demons you are holding in here are going to keep on haunting you until you talk about them.*

He pocketed the keys, climbed out of the truck and went into the shop. The bell over the door let out a happy little jingle as he entered. His gaze didn't go to the desserts in the case, though, instead it lingered on a pencil drawing tacked to the wall. In the window to the right hung the single gold star flag. Jack swallowed hard and fought the urge to flee.

"Jack Barlow! So nice to see you!" Betty came out from behind the counter to greet him with a warm, generous hug he didn't deserve.

"Good afternoon, Miz Delacorte," Jack said. He stepped out of her embrace and tried to work a smile to his face. It didn't work.

"It's so nice to see you home, safe and sound. Though I will admit that seeing you makes me miss my boy something fierce." Her eyes misted, and her smile wobbled. "I'm glad you were there with him."

"Miz Delacorte…" Jack shook his head. What was he supposed to say? *I wasn't there for him when he needed me? I led him in the wrong direction, and that got him killed?*

"Now, don't you start feeling bad that you're the one who came home. The Lord has His plans, and it's not for me to say why or what for. For whatever reason, He needed my Eli home in heaven, and at least I know up there, my sweet boy isn't scared or hurting or anything."

Jack's gaze flicked again to the pencil drawing. Guilt clawed at him, the panther he had tried to avoid for so long becoming bigger, stronger, meaner. *Jack* was the reason that this wonderful woman's son was cold in the ground instead of here with her. *Jack* had been in charge—and *Jack* had failed as a leader. He hadn't just failed his troops, he'd failed his best friend. "Miz Delacorte, I'm sorry about Eli. I…" Again, the words clogged in his throat.

"I can see this is upsetting you." Betty gave his chest a little pat. "And I'm sure you didn't come here to talk to me about things that are over and done. So what can I get for you?"

The coward in him leaped at the change in subject. He cleared his throat. "Uh, Meri sent me. She wants… one of everything."

"One of everything? Oh, my." Betty's wide face broke into a generous smile. She bustled behind the counter and set about boxing up the sweet treats. "Well, it's about time. If you ask me, that girl spent too much time looking through the glass case instead of enjoying what's inside."

By the time Betty was done, she had filled four large white boxes with cupcakes, brownies, cookies, chocolates and all kinds of things Jack couldn't name. He started to reach for his wallet, but Betty waved it away.

"On the house. For you, for what you did, watching over my Eli when he was there, and for Meri, who deserves all these and more." She placed the boxes in his hands, then gave him a soft kiss on the cheek.

Jack mumbled something that sounded like a thank-you, then got back in his truck and hated himself for letting Betty Delacorte think he was some kind of hero. It was a good long while before he put it in gear and drove back to Meri's cottage. He dropped the boxes on her front porch, then headed home, like the coward he was.

Meri slid out of bed and padded barefoot down the hall. She glanced out the window at Grandpa Ray's cottage, mere feet away from her own. His window was open, the lights off, and if she held her breath, she could barely catch the even sound of his soft snores. Maybe it was her imagination or stubborn hope, but she thought he sounded better than when she'd first arrived two weeks ago.

That gave her hope for the future. Maybe if Grandpa kept taking his medications and kept on eating right and doing the daily walks she'd instituted, he could get better. She wasn't naive enough to think Grandpa would live forever, but she'd at least like a few more years. Grandpa Ray was the closest thing she had to a real parent, and she'd always pictured him walking her down the aisle, holding his first great-grandchild, sitting on her porch and watching the sun go down over the world.

She realized, though, that once Grandpa Ray was better, she would have no reason to stay in Stone Gap. She had a job waiting for her in New York, a career that had barely gotten its wings, and she needed to get back there. Get back to her dreams.

Get her life back together, period.

She thought of the camera up in her room, gathering

dust. Maybe tomorrow she'd take it and go down to the water. Try to snap a few pictures.

Maybe.

In the kitchen, Meri opened the first box of desserts from Aunt Betty's bakery. She didn't know why Jack had just dropped them off and gone home. She'd called his house, but gotten no answer, and when she'd asked Grandpa Ray about Jack leaving earlier, he told her that Jack was a man who needed space sometimes.

Best thing to do is give him that space. Eventually, he'll get to feeling lonely and he'll come back around to living in the world again. He's just having trouble feeling like he belongs.

She knew that feeling, knew it well. Though why Jack Barlow—war hero, town bachelor, loyal son and friend—would feel like that, she didn't know.

She grabbed the box, pulled on a sweatshirt, then headed out to sit on the Adirondack chair. She settled on the hard wooden seat, the box on her lap, and was bringing the first bite of a raspberry thumbprint cookie to her lips when she saw a familiar figure cutting a long, straight path across the placid surface of the lake.

Meri put aside the box, then picked her way down the path to the water. The full moon above her lit her way, casting its pale light across Jack's back, glinting off his arms as he raised them, then dug in again, swimming hard and fast. His arms were long, sleek machines in the water, pulling his body through the dark surface with easy, swift strokes.

By the time she reached the bank, he had paused, treading water, his breath coming in fast, short gasps. After a moment, he started toward shore. He rose up, a magnificent-looking man, the water glistening across the ridges and planes of his muscular body. She took in a breath, but still her heart skipped a beat and her pulse thundered in her veins.

She'd been talking about decadence and fantasies earlier, as if she meant chocolates and cookies, when really, her biggest fantasy was a six-foot-two, sleek, wet, all-American male stud. *Holy cow.*

"Meri? What are you doing out here?"

"Uh…couldn't sleep." She held up the half-eaten cookie as if that explained everything.

"Me neither." He cast a glance at the ground, then let out a soft curse.

"What?"

"Forgot a towel."

She grinned. "You were in that much of a rush to take a swim?"

"Sometimes, yeah, I am." He shook his head, sending a soft spray of water in an outward arc.

Meri put the cookie on a stump, then unzipped her sweatshirt and handed it to Jack. "Here."

"I can't take that."

"You prefer to stand there and freeze to death?"

"No, I just don't want to take a jacket from…"

"From a girl?" She propped her opposite fist on her hip and shook the jacket at him. "Don't be a gentleman at the cost of being an idiot, Jack."

He stepped forward, so close she could see the water droplets glistening on his skin, reflecting the moonlight in tiny oval diamonds. The cool air made steam rise off his warm body, and a part of her ached to touch that steam, to let her hand trail down his arms, his chest, his legs. "What about you?" he said.

"What…what about me?"

"Aren't you going to be cold?"

"I'm…" Her gaze roamed over his body again before she jerked her attention back to his face. "I'm quite warm right now."

A knowing smile slid across his face and he shifted even closer. "You have changed, Meri Prescott."

"I keep telling you that."

"The Meri I remember wasn't so…bold." He trailed a finger down her lips, over her chin, down her neck, lingering above her cleavage. "The Meri I remember would blush at the mere mention of sex."

"I don't blush anymore, Jack."

"Oh, I bet I could make you blush."

She raised her chin, her heart thudding so hard in her chest she was sure half of Stone Gap could hear the rapid *thud-thud-thud*. "I'd like to see you try."

His finger, cool against her skin, slipped over the ridge of her V-neck and slowly drew a lazy line between her breasts. Her nipples, without the barrier of a bra, tightened against the thin cotton. Jack smiled, then leaned in until his lips were brushing against hers. "Do you still close your eyes when you kiss?"

"Only one way to find out." She'd hoped he would join her on her dessert gorgefest/picnic. And hoped that maybe, after the rush to have the treats, she could indulge in him, too. Fulfill the fantasies that had starred in her dreams ever since her first real date with Jack.

But then he had ducked out without a word, leaving the boxes on her porch and leaving her wondering if maybe she was fantasizing about the wrong man. But here he was, in the flesh, and what amazing flesh it was. Hot enough to make her forget the boxes on her porch and the missed picnic.

"Do you want to find out?" she asked.

"I have wanted to know the answer to that question for two weeks," he murmured. He kissed her, hot, fiery, hard and fast, his mouth opening against hers like a hunger too long denied. Her body responded like quicksilver, surging against his, heat racing through her veins, into her core. The sweatshirt tumbled to the ground and Meri reached for Jack, her hands sliding against the cool slipperiness of his wet skin.

He groaned and lowered his touch to her back, then over her buttocks, drawing her pelvis up and into his erection. She wanted him and she wanted him now.

"Jack," she whispered, into his mouth, against his tongue, a whisper that became a plea the second time. "Jack."

His hands snaked beneath her T-shirt and up to cup her breasts. The cool touch made her nipples harden instantly, and fire erupted deep inside her gut. He nudged the shirt upward and an instant later, her breasts were exposed to the air, to his touch, to a naughty deliciousness of being outside, in the dark.

She ran her hands down his back, then under the elastic banding of his swimsuit. His skin was cooler here, which only encouraged her touch, around his hard, tight butt, then sliding one hand around the front to grasp his erection and slide her hand along its length.

Jack let out a sharp breath, then a curse. He stepped back and her hand slid off him and out of his shorts. Her shirt fluttered back down into place. "I'm sorry. I shouldn't have done this. I'm not…"

"It's okay, Jack. I'm not sixteen anymore. I know what sex is. And how to have it." She grinned and stepped toward him, but he moved back again.

"I'm not..." He let out a curse again. "I'm not inter-ested in you that way."

He might as well have thrown her into the lake. She sputtered in surprise. How had she read the signals so wrong? What had she missed? "But you...you kissed me. Twice. And then this...whatever that just was."

"They were just kisses, Meri. Not a relationship."

The hurt stung, like a blade slicing along her heart, but she raised her chin, defiant, cool. "Who the hell said I wanted a relationship?"

He moved into her space, his dark eyes meeting hers. Heat curled between them. "Are you telling me you want a fling? One night with the guy who might have been all those years ago? One screw for old times' sake?"

Her eyes burned but she refused to let Jack know he had hurt her. "You might think you're doing a great job with this jerk-of-the-year act, Jack, but I'm not buying it. I know you. Better than you think. And you are not this—" she waved a hand between them "—arrogant bastard."

"Maybe you're the one that's wrong. Maybe this is who I was all along."

Maybe that was so. Maybe she had idealized and ro-manticized their past and had never seen the real Jack Barlow. She bent down, picked up the sweatshirt, then pressed it to his chest. "Better cover up before your icy heart freezes to a stop."

Chapter Eleven

Icy heart.

Those two words stayed with Jack. Stayed like a thorn in his thumb. She didn't know. She didn't understand. And he wasn't about to slice open that slab of iceberg sitting in his chest and explain what had changed.

He pounded through the streets of Stone Gap, ignoring the heat of the rising sun, the thick humidity that forced his lungs to work overtime. He ran, down streets, in and out of parks, through parking lots. He ran and ran, as if a demon was chasing him.

He hadn't paid attention to his path or his route. Partly because he knew Stone Gap like the back of his hand, and partly because he'd figured he'd run until the words *icy heart* stopped ringing in his head. Then he rounded a corner, and his steps faltered, and the masochistic side of him laughed.

The Stone Gap cemetery loomed in front of him, its wrought-iron gates propped open, revealing a shady, flower-lined path that curved like a mistress.

He cursed, and lowered his head. But when he tried to power forward, to run past it like he had the mailbox on Juniper Street and the bike rack at the Publix, his feet refused to go straight. Instead, his steps veered right, off the sidewalk and down that shady path.

He didn't need a map. Didn't need a guide. He knew where to turn, which of the winding paths to take. He hadn't been inside this cemetery in more than five years, not since his grandmother's funeral, but it was as if he'd been here yesterday.

A hill crested in front of him, lush green lawn leading up to a rhododendron that had gotten overgrown. At the back stood a thick, tall oak tree, its branches spreading like arms over the granite stones beneath its shade.

A stone mausoleum stood to the right of the tree. It dominated the hill and the landscape with its ornate carved angels perched atop pillars that sat on three granite steps. Stone flowerpots held blooming annuals, so well-tended not a single bloom had faded. Letters carved into the top generations ago were beginning to darken with age, but the name was clear.

PRESCOTT.

Beside it, a smaller gravestone, still shiny and unblemished, less elaborate and far more simple, reading DELACORTE. The families flanking each other in death as they did in life.

Jack took a step. Something crunched under his foot, and he froze. His heart stilled, his breath held. His brain whirred like an engine skipping a beat. It was a stick, just a stick.

But his mind didn't see or hear *stick*. In Jack's mind, the snap had been a mine, a trigger tripped by a careless footstep. *Get down, get down*, his mind screamed.

He clenched his fists. Forced a breath in. Out. Another. There was no danger here. He was safe. There were no troops behind him, no men waiting for him to signal their next move. Nothing but a shady oak tree that had lost a branch. He was safe.

Then he glanced up the hill again, at the small, simple stone with Eli's name etched across the front.

Jack wasn't safe. Far from it.

The reminder of her promise came in the form of a monogrammed envelope with a giant gold *AL* intertwined with a smaller *P*. Heavy hand-cut linen cardstock—the kind of paper Meri's mother used for important occasions.

Hidden meaning—*don't ignore this*.

Meri was half tempted to just toss the invitation in the trash. She held it out separate from the rest of the mail as she headed back up the walk to Grandpa Ray's house. She glanced around for Jack, but he hadn't been by in days.

Was he avoiding her after what had happened that night at the lake? The Jack she remembered had never run from a problem—he'd always gone headfirst into everything he tried. It was part of what had made him so perfect for the military. But this Jack, this wounded man who had returned, seemed to do the opposite. Jack Barlow had become an enigma, one that intrigued her and drove her crazy all at the same time. True to his word, he had fixed her car, driving it off to the shop one morning and returning it ten times better than before. She wasn't sure what all he had done, but the aged Toyota purred like a kitten now and sported four new tires. He wouldn't take a dime of payment, just dropped off the keys and told her to drive safe. Because he was her friend? More? Or because he was just being a good neighbor? Either way, she should forget him—the problem was getting that message to her brain.

From his seat on the porch swing, Grandpa nodded toward her as she climbed the porch stairs. "I see from the fancy-dancy envelope you're holding that Her Majesty is requesting your presence."

"She wants me to photograph one of her events." She handed over Grandpa Ray's pile of junk mail, then took a seat on the space beside him. "The new LL Bean catalog came in the mail for you today."

"Just what I need. Another flannel shirt." He grinned, then gestured toward the white envelope. "You at least going to open the summons?"

"I'm not even sure if I'm going. I still haven't picked up my camera or managed to take a single photo." She blew her hair out of her face. "Besides, I don't know if I want to deal with all my mother's stuffy friends."

"What better way to start taking pictures again than at the zoo?" Grandpa winked.

Meri swallowed a laugh. "That's not nice."

"I've been to your mother's parties. It's like watching a safari. All those animals, trying to either kill or outdo the others." Grandpa Ray nodded at the envelope. "If I can eat salad, you can go to your mother's shindig."

"Are you comparing eating healthy to dealing with my mother?"

"They're almost the same thing, aren't they?" Grandpa Ray grinned. "Your momma can be as irritating as a billy goat in a bad mood, but that doesn't mean you're supposed to ignore her. Blood is blood, after all. And besides, she's finally taking an interest in you doing something other than looking pretty and wearing one of those crown things…"

"Tiara."

"Tee-hee foolishness, if you ask me. If she can take an interest, then you can at least help her out with a few snapshots."

Meri toyed with the envelope. She bit her lower lip, then finally let out a sigh. "You're right."

"That's one of the perks of being the oldest man alive."

She nudged him with her elbow. "You are not the oldest man alive. Heck, you're not even the oldest man in Stone Gap."

"Tell that to my knees and my ticker." When she shot a look of concern his way, Grandpa Ray smiled and patted her hand. "I'm just fine, Merry Girl. Thanks to those salads and vegetables."

She laughed. "Okay, okay. Hint taken." She slid a finger under the flap and lifted the thick paper, then slid out the single square sheet inside. "Well, it's definitely not a backyard barbecue. Apparently, she wants to celebrate the first day of summer with an outdoor extravaganza. There will be a dance floor, a band and—"

"The regular Prescott simple shindig accoutrements."

Meri laughed. "I don't think I've ever heard you use the word *accoutrements*."

"Hey, just because I live like a hermit in the woods doesn't mean I can't dazzle with a few big words here and there." He tipped his head toward her. "It pays to do the crossword puzzle once in a while."

Meri pressed a kiss to her grandfather's cheek then got to her feet. "I'm glad you're feeling better."

"Me, too. That means you can get back to your life and stop hanging around here, keeping an old man company."

"I haven't minded one bit," Meri said. She looked out over the woods beside them, the curve of the road that led away from her beloved lake and toward the road that would take her back to New York. "Besides, I'm not quite sure what life it is that I'm going back to. Exactly."

"You have to go," Luke said on Friday afternoon. He stood in the shaded interior of the garage while Jack finished cleaning up the work spaces. Their father had gone home early, feeling a bit taxed by his first full week back at work, and Jack had offered to lock up. A few minutes after five, Luke had shown up out of the blue to shoot the breeze and get his oil changed. Jack had put him to work sweeping the floor, but thus far Luke had done a lot of talking and not a lot of sweeping. "You are my plus one."

Jack scowled. The last thing he wanted to do was go to some overglorified, overdressed barbecue. "Plus ones are for a date. With a woman. An actual woman, I might add, not a department-store mannequin."

"That was only once. And just so I could take the high-speed highway lane. You gotta admit, it was pretty hilarious."

Jack arched a brow. "Not when you took my car to do it."

Luke just grinned. "I'm more mature now. Note I said more mature, not actually mature."

"Duly noted." Jack wiped the grease off his hands, then tossed the rag onto his tool bench. He gestured toward Luke's car, still sitting in the bay. "Oil's changed. I topped off the fluids and changed out your air filter. You might want to think about replacing those spark plugs next time you come in."

"I'm smart enough to tell when you are changing the subject." Luke fished the invitation out of his pocket and waved it at Jack. "So, how about it? You going?"

"Why the hell would I want to go to a Prescott garden party? When have I ever gone to a Prescott garden party?"

"When you were seventeen and trying to impress Meri. Even wore that long skinny tie that you thought was so stylish."

He'd felt the disapproving glare of Anna Lee Prescott the entire time. Meri had spent the whole party meeting sponsors and supporters for her pageants, leaving Jack feeling more out of place than the waitstaff. "And it was a mistake."

"Going to the party or wearing the tie?"

"Both."

"All the more reason to rectify your fashion idiocy and come with me this time. I'll even help you pick out your clothes."

"For one, I am old enough to dress myself." Jack pulled open the tool chest drawers and started sorting the day's tools into their proper places. "For another, why the hell would you go to this thing anyway? And why were you invited?"

"Because of my new business venture."

"Business venture?" Jack finished sorting the sockets and moved on to the screwdrivers. "You mean, something other than living off the family dime?"

His brother shot him a glare. "Remember Dexter Cornwell?"

Jack nodded. "Spoiled kid in high school."

"Spoiled *rich* kid. He called me last week, wanting to fill some positions at his events company. He started a business a few years back planning weddings and it mushroomed into everything from bar mitzvahs to dog birthdays."

"You're taking a job helping a poodle blow out its candles?"

Luke scowled. "It's more than that."

Jack laughed, then shut the last drawer on the tool chest and fished Luke's keys out of his pocket. "Have fun at the garden party. Watch out for the Chihuahuas." He headed toward the door connecting the garage to the office. It was getting late, and he wanted to head down to Ray's to finish up those last few chores. And if there weren't any chores left to do, Jack would find something to occupy the hours between now and midnight. Maybe then he could sleep and stop dreaming about Meri, ending that constant craving she had awakened in him.

"Jack?"

He turned back at Luke's voice. "Yeah?"

"I think you need to go to this thing. You need to get back out in the world."

"I am out in the world."

"Spending your days either under a Chevy or chopping wood for Ray isn't getting out in the world. It's been a year since you came home. When are you really going to be home?"

Home. It had been a hell of a long time since Jack had felt anything like that. He'd tried, Lord knew he'd tried, since he'd returned to Stone Gap. But he had found nothing but an aching, painful emptiness in all the places that had once brought him joy. It was as if a black-and-white cloud had been dropped over the world he once saw in Technicolor.

There had been moments, with Meri, when he'd glimpsed that Technicolor world again, but then he would remember and it would all disappear.

Eli would never see, never enjoy that world again. He'd never hear the call of a bird, feel the kiss of a woman. And that, Jack knew, was why he couldn't come all the way home. Why he could do nothing more than...exist.

"You know what you need, Jack? To enjoy yourself for once. And stop wallowing in this pit." Luke grabbed his shoulder and met his gaze head-on. "It's not a crime to live, you know."

Jack didn't answer his brother. He just stepped through the doorway and with a screech of metal, shut him out.

Chapter Twelve

Meri waited until after Grandpa Ray had eaten supper and settled down for the night in his recliner with a new episode of *Ax Men* on TV to watch, then headed back to her cottage, grabbed her camera and headed outside into the waning light. As she did, she noticed the label she had affixed to the camera's body the day she got her business cards.

Photography by Meri Prescott.

Those words had made it real. They'd been the first step toward her thinking she could be something else, do something else. And she'd be damned if she was going to let some mugger take it from her.

Tomorrow she had her first photography job since the attack. Okay, not really a paid job, but either way, doing her job meant getting behind the camera again.

The sun was setting over the lake, kissing the dark

water with hues of pink and purple. A loon called from somewhere in the distance, and the bullfrogs began their evening song. A pair of ducks swam a lazy path toward the small island in the center of the lake.

She raised the viewfinder to her right eye. The edge of the camera brushed against her scar, and it seemed to sear through the skin. Meri drew in a deep breath, held it, let it go. She tried again, but when she looked through the eyepiece, she saw nothing but a blur of images. A New York City street, a graffiti display that had caught her eye, its myriad of colors twirling into a spray-painted image of a landscape, art created by a kid in the dark of night, on a giant canvas. Then a dark shadow moving in front of her lens, and Meri started to say something, asking the person to move, to wait, and then before she could say anything, the camera was yanked away and she found herself against the wall with a knife to her throat.

She dropped the camera and let it dangle from her neck. Then she lowered to her knees and put her head in her hands. She was okay; she was in Stone Gap. She wasn't on that street. Why had she thought she could do this?

"You okay?"

Jack. That was whom she'd seen through the viewfinder. Not the mugger. Meri jerked her head up. "Yeah, yeah. I'm fine. You scared me."

"I'm sorry. I thought you saw me." He reached out, took her hand and tugged her to her feet. "What's the matter?"

"I'm fine."

"No, you're not. And trust me, I'm the expert on saying you're fine when you're not." He gestured toward the camera. "What are you trying to do?"

"Get my life back," she said softly, then she sighed and took the camera off her neck. "But it's harder than I thought. I don't know why I keep trying to do this. Maybe I should just give this photography thing up and go work at a fast-food place or something."

"Why would you give up what you love?"

She raised her gaze to his, and thought of that day in Gator's Garage. "Because sometimes what you love doesn't love you back."

"Then maybe you're not trying hard enough."

"I've been trying." She blew her hair out of her face. "Lord knows I've tried a hundred times since that day."

He let out a short sound of disbelief.

"What?" Meri asked.

"I have a 'that day,' too. And nothing's been the same for me either."

She wanted to ask what had happened, what had impacted him so much, but she didn't want to push Jack. He'd opened the door a little, and she knew it would be far better for him to welcome her in than for her to barge her way in to his world. "Then maybe we both need to try harder."

He reached over and lifted the camera toward her. "What better time to start than the present?"

She caught his blue eyes and saw support in there, caring. He was right—what better time than the present to finally conquer these nightmares. She'd come out here, determined not to let that mugger get one more day's space in her mind, and that meant she needed to keep on trying. So she raised the camera, aiming toward the moonlight cascading over the lake, and talked to Jack while she lined up the simple shot. *No pressure, an easy shot, let the camera do the work.*

"Everyone told me I should have talked about what happened to me, gone to therapy, all that stuff." She held the shot, then blinked, trying to clear her mind of the visions from before. She was at the lake, seeing the beauty of the water, the moonlight. Meri exhaled, then pressed the shutter button. *Click.* One shot done. "They said I should have told someone other than the cops and the doctors, but I didn't. I kept saying I was fine, I was dealing with it, but—" she took another picture, a third, not caring about exposure or aperture or anything other than just pointing and clicking, and the little feeling of success that grew in her with each image filling her memory card "—clearly I wasn't."

"You're dealing now."

"One shot at a time." She grinned, then raised the camera in his direction. "What about you?"

"What about me?"

"What are you doing to get over that day?" She focused the camera on Jack's face, but he stepped out of range. "Hey!"

He closed the distance between them, until the view through the camera showed only a blur of his face, and she gave up on trying to capture his image. "You know what the remedy is for dealing with stuff you don't want to deal with?"

She shook her head. He reached over her neck and lifted the camera, then put it down on the stump beside them.

"Skinny-dipping."

She laughed. Her chest was light, her heart happy. It was a perfect night, the Nikon was finally edging away from enemy and back to friend again, and she was finding her steps along the right path again. "You're crazy, Jack. There's no such thing as skinny-dipping therapy."

"There's water therapy. And that's the same thing. Practically."

"Water therapy?"

"Yup. Football players do it all the time."

"For injuries of their body, not their brain. And that involves ice." She shivered. "I have no desire to sit in a tub of ice."

"But you do have the desire to slip into a nice cool lake on a hot early-summer night, don't you?"

The word *desire* made her go warm deep in her gut. Had her hormones screaming, *yes, yes, let's do that*. She forgot all about taking pictures, all about her job. Slipping into a cool lake with Jack Barlow…yes, that was a damned good idea. "Jack, I don't know if I should—"

"Besides, you owe me. Remember our bet in the fishing boat? Whoever catches the most fish wins? I caught a fish and you caught how many? None." He came closer to her, the heat of his body wafting over them and luring her into his smile. "That means you still owe me a dip in the lake. Naked."

"I thought that bet was called off due to inclement weather."

He grinned. "That was just a rain delay. And tonight—" he glanced up at the sky, the smile widening on his face and turning into a tease "—there's not a cloud in the sky."

"You just want to see me naked." She put a fist on her hip, pretending that she didn't desperately want to see him naked, too. That night on the lake last week, when she'd run her hands over his wet, sleek body—that had been awesome. She wasn't sure she was strong enough to stand a repeat of that event without jumping Jack's bones.

"For purely therapeutic reasons only."

She laughed. How she wanted to resist him, to forget him, but she couldn't. All her life, it was as if Jack Barlow had had this hold on her heart, and whenever he had teased her out of a bad mood or tempted her into doing something dangerous, she became putty in his hands. "Oh, so now you're a doctor?"

"I am if you need a thorough internal exam."

Oh, she needed that. In a bad way. She'd been needing that from Jack Barlow for years. Maybe it was the fantasy of the unknown, the mystery of what could have been if they hadn't broken up. Ever since her first date with Jack, she'd wondered what it would be like to make love with him. And now, with the carnal knowledge of an adult, her fantasies had gone further, filling her dreams with images of his naked body on top of hers, behind hers, inside hers.

She was here to heal, to find herself again, she'd told him. Maybe part of that was finally giving herself the things she had delayed and denied for so long.

Not things. *Thing*, singular. As in a hunky, six-foot-two man who was battling his own demons. A man like that wouldn't want anything more from her—he'd made that clear a thousand times already—and that was exactly what Meri wanted, too. No strings, no attachments, nothing to bind her to this town that she both loved and despised.

To take that risk, leap off into the unknown and, yes, skinny-dip, as scary as it sounded. Get naked, get in the water and live those parts of life she had never been able to before.

"You know what they say about therapy," she said to him, her gaze meeting his blue eyes, seeming almost black now in the dim light. "It's best when it's shared." She tugged on the hem of her T-shirt and pulled it over her head, then tossed it on the ground.

Jack's gaze dropped to the lacy white bra she wore. He cleared his throat. "I don't think I've ever heard that, but it sounds legit."

"Totally." She grinned. "So, are you going to join me, Doctor?"

By the time Jack got his shorts unbuttoned, Meri was already making a dash for the water. Her round, firm ass seemed to wink at him in the moonlight, and in a splash it was gone. Well, hell, she had gone and gotten totally naked. He'd thought she would back out at the last second, but Meri had dived in—literally—the whole way. He kicked off his boxers, then took off after her.

He'd tried avoiding her, staying as far away from Ray's property as he could, but it hadn't worked. Jack was drawn to Meri, over and over again, like a bee to a flower. If anything, being away from her put her in his thoughts more than ever. Maybe his brother was right. Maybe he needed to enjoy himself for once. With Meri.

He watched Meri's naked body sliding through the water of Stone Gap Lake, and in half a second, Jack stopped thinking about anything other than how fast he could be out there with her, too. The water hit him like an iceberg, but the warm air above took the edge off the cold. That, and the knowledge that a very naked, very slippery Meri was a few feet away. He did a quick breast-stroke out farther into the lake, then treaded water in front of her. "You didn't wait for my answer."

"I was pretty sure you'd follow. Naked woman in the water? That's a no-brainer for any guy with a pulse."

"I wouldn't jump in a cold lake naked for just any woman, you know," Jack said.

"Are you saying I'm special?" A tease lit her face, sparked in her eyes.

"More than you know," he said quietly. Damn, where had that come from? He hadn't meant to say it out loud—hell, hadn't even meant for it to go past his brain. So he did what any guy afraid of commitment would do—he splashed her and passed it off as a joke. "After all, you're still the only girl in Stone Gap to climb to the top of the Old Man."

"Oh, my God, I totally forgot about that. I got in so much trouble for climbing that tree. My mother grounded me for a month after she saw how skinned up my knees got."

"I still can't believe you did it. What were you thinking?"

"That I was thirteen and hopelessly infatuated with my cousin's best friend."

That was news to him. Meri had been infatuated with him when she was young? "You were?"

"Oh, come on. You had to know." She rolled her eyes. "For Pete's sake, half the girls in Stone Gap were infatuated with you, Jack Barlow. The other half were infatuated with your brothers. You come from some good-looking stock."

He swam a little closer to her, so close he could glimpse the pale lines of her limbs and the soft globes of her breasts beneath the water's surface, and that had him imagining those legs wrapped around him, her arms sliding along his back. "You think I'm good-looking?"

"I always thought you were good-looking. I dated you, remember?"

"I remember, Meri. I remember very well."

They had only dated for a year, a relationship they had kind of fallen into. For years they'd been friends, traveling in a pack with Eli and other mutual friends. Then one day it had been just Jack and Meri, and by the end of the night he'd kissed her. That had changed everything.

"Then you should also remember that *you* were the one who didn't want me." She gave him a little splash and backed up a few feet.

"Who says I didn't want you?"

"You did. That day in your dad's garage. When you told me that you wanted someone with more depth than a princess who trotted around on the stage in high heels." She shook her head and turned away, then forced a smile to her face. "And then you went away, and that was all she wrote."

He'd been a jerk that day, and knew it. He remembered every detail, and back then, in the foolish naïveté of the young, he'd thought he was doing Meri a favor.

He remembered the way the sun had been streaming in through the garage windows, glinting off Meri's blond hair like strands of gold. She'd been beautiful, but then again, she'd always been beautiful. He remembered wondering where the real Meri was, because she'd turned into a facade of herself over the year he'd dated her, sinking more and more into that pageant world of false eyelashes and false smiles. And he'd told himself he was better off without this Meri in his life, because then he could concentrate on the military and not get distracted.

But the Meri who had returned to Stone Gap was real. It was as if by peeling away all the layers of makeup and glittery gowns, he'd seen the woman he'd been looking for years ago. That intrigued him, and with her naked in the water beside him, it made him wonder what else had grown up about Meri.

"Seems to me, if we're here swimming naked together, that isn't all she wrote," Jack said. "And in case you haven't noticed, I still want you, Meri."

If he'd hoped that she would just swim into his arms and answer this pounding need in his body, he'd been wrong. Instead she put a little more distance between them. "Then why did you break up with me? Was it just because of the pageants?"

"That was part of it, but not the whole reason." He couldn't keep hiding his feelings and thoughts forever. It hadn't gotten him anywhere but sitting alone on his porch, drinking beer and beating himself up. "And I've been sorry ever since." He met her gaze. "I'm sorry, Meri."

She looked away. "It was a long time ago."

"Maybe so, but it doesn't mean I haven't been a jerk a few dozen times, starting with that day. I broke up with you because I had this weird superstition that if I had someone waiting for me back home, it meant I would die in some godforsaken country. I told myself it would be better for you, and for me, if I wasn't attached to anyone."

"That's silly."

He shrugged. "Most soldiers have superstitions. They wear a lucky pair of socks or carry a lucky coin."

"And for you, your superstition was no unlucky connections?"

Now that she put it that way, it did sound silly. The one thing he had craved when he was overseas was the very connections he had left behind. The voices, the faces of those he loved. "Yeah. You're right, it was silly. I should have known better. And I should have kept you in my life."

"I don't think it was silly. I think it was sweet." She swam up to him and draped her arms around his neck. Her legs brushed his every few seconds. The hurt had ebbed in her features and a smile curved her lips. He'd always liked that about Meri, how quick she was to forgive, to move forward. "You are a very sweet man, Jack Barlow."

"I was going for smoldering and dangerous."

Her leg trailed along his and sparked nerve endings on every inch of its path. "Oh, you are that, and much more."

"Not me," he said, shaking his head. "You are the smoldering, dangerous one."

A slow, sexy smile curved up her face. "You're just trying to butter me up."

"And what would I be trying to butter you up for?"

She took in a breath, like this was a big step, admitting the truth. The breath raised her chest, giving him a too-brief peek of her nipples. "Taking advantage of my naked state."

"The thought never occurred to me." He affected an innocent tone, but inside his brain, his hormones were staging a mutiny against common sense.

She laughed, a light sound that seemed to carry on the breeze and nestle in his chest. "Liar."

"What makes you think I'm lying?" He slid his legs along hers, then roamed his hands down her breasts, over her hips. She let out a little gasp but didn't move away, didn't stop him. She was like silk beneath his touch, and he couldn't seem to stop touching her, feeling her. All he wanted was to slip inside her. "Because I'm totally not thinking about sex right now."

"Really? Neither am I." Meri hesitated only a second, then she slipped her right hand under the water, and trailed along his belly. She grabbed his erection and let her palm slide up and down.

Electricity arced in his veins and he groaned, aching with need for her. He wrapped one leg around hers, pinning her body against his, but it made them bob under the water and pop back up, sputtering and laughing. "We could drown doing this in the deep water."

"Then maybe we should take it a little…inland."

They swam toward the shore until their feet touched the soft bottom of the lake. The houses around the lake were dark, the residents gone to bed, and the only light came from the moon above them. Jack had told himself not to get involved with Meri, not to get close to Meri, but she was the only thing that seemed right in his world.

Just one night, he told himself. *Just one.* Then she would go back to New York and he'd go back to burying himself in work and chores and sweat equity, and he would never have to tell her about Eli and THAT DAY.

One night.

Was it selfish of him to want that?

When she slid her hand along his erection again, he stopped debating and took action instead. He lowered his mouth to hers, his hands going to her back, sliding down to cup her ass and haul her body against his. He deepened the kiss, dancing with her tongue.

It was all hands and legs and bodies, a slippery, sliding, amazing frenzy to touch, to feel, to have her. Jack cupped her breasts, letting his thumbs drift over her firm, hard nipples. She gasped, arched against him, raising one leg as she did. He slid into her in one easy, fast move. She called out his name, and in that moment, Jack was a goner.

He hoisted her weight in his hands while she wrapped her arms around his neck and leaned back into his palms, allowing him deeper access. The dark night covered them from view, and the warm water amplified every stroke.

Pleasure, pure pleasure. That was all Jack felt as he made love to Meri. The past he had been running from disappeared in those sweet, hot moments between them. His mind emptied of everything but her, listening to her soft mews, then hearing her gasp, feeling her clutch at him as he increased his strokes and she called out his name again, this time in one long, aching breath. His world exploded and he came inside her, in a wonderful, breathless release that for just a minute washed away the pain that crowded his every thought.

Chapter Thirteen

Five seconds after she arrived, Meri regretted her decision. She was wearing a pale pink dress she hated, makeup that felt like a mask. She had curled her hair and left it down around her shoulders, but sprayed the strands within an inch of their life to keep the style from bending to the hot, humid air.

Her mother crossed the lawn with effortless strides, having somehow managed the walking-in-heels-on-grass thing years ago. Meri had chosen flats for today, the dressiest option she had that also allowed her to move freely.

"I'm so glad you came, Meredith," her mother said. "It'll be so delightful for people to catch up with you."

"I'm here to take pictures, Momma." Meri raised the camera as evidence and snapped a few wide shots of the party, then a close-up of one of the floral arrangements on a nearby cocktail table. Working would keep her from thinking about last night with Jack, about their sweet, delicious, wonderful lovemaking in the water. She'd gone to sleep thinking about Jack, woken up thinking about Jack and spent half the morning daydreaming about Jack. They'd made plans to meet tonight for a picnic by the lake, and she could hardly wait for that hour to arrive. "I plan on working, not socializing."

Her mother waved away the sentence. "A lady doesn't *work*, Meredith Lee. She *attends*."

Attends? A shiver of foreboding slithered along Meri's spine. All the right things were in place for one of her mother's parties: the carefully arranged finger foods tended by tuxedoed waitstaff; the polite, demure waitresses handing out mimosas and champagne; the colorful flower arrangements designed not to overpower the tables yet still make an impact.

"I'm here for professional reasons only. Remember?"

"Of course, of course. And you will take your pictures. But first I wanted you to say hello to Bert Mathers." Anna Lee took Meri's elbow and began detouring her toward the buffet table. "You remember him, don't you, dear?"

Meri stopped walking. "Bert? What is he doing here?"

The pieces jigsawed into place. Meri glanced around and recognized the director of the first pageant she had competed in, her coach during the years she'd competed nationally, the designer who had created Meri's custom glittery dresses. Across the lawn stood Dexter Cornwell, who had taken over his father's events company, talking to Luke Barlow. Beside them were two other coaches in the industry and Bert's assistant. At least ninety percent of the people in attendance worked in the pageant arena in one way or another.

"What is going on?" Meri asked.

"Oh, and look," Anna Lee went on. "There's Harvey Stills. You remember him, don't you, Meredith Lee? He's that plastic surgeon out of Charleston." Her mother leaned in, as if she was sharing a privileged secret. "He comes highly recommended."

"To fix imperfections?" Outrage exploded in her chest. "Is that why you invited him? So you can make me perfect again?"

Her mother pursed her lips. "I merely thought you might like to be…restored."

Restored? As if she was some kind of dented antique that needed a new finish before it could be displayed? "What the hell is this about? Why am I really here?"

Anna Lee gasped. "A lady does not curse, Meredith Lee. Now try not to slouch and don't forget to smile. These people have worked very hard to help get you where you are today."

Meri refused to move. She flung off her mother's hand. "You haven't listened to a word I've said, have you? I don't think you've listened to anything I've said since the day I was born. I don't want to go back to pageants. I don't want to compete. I don't want to smile nice and walk tall and pretend my shoes aren't killing my feet."

Anna Lee let out a little laugh. "Who said anything about competing? I merely thought you would like to be involved again. Maybe in coaching or judging. After all, this was such a big part of your life. I can imagine how hard it was to walk away." Anna Lee patted Meri's hand. "If you're worried about how people will react to you after you dropped out of Miss America—"

"I didn't drop out, Momma. I *ran* away. Ran as far as I could go. Because I knew if I didn't, you'd keep on shoving me into those pageants until the day I died."

"You just had a little breakdown. I pushed you too hard." Anna Lee flicked her wrist as if that made the past disappear. "That's neither here nor there. You are here now."

"Because you asked me to be, Momma. Because I thought you finally cared about what I did and what made me happy." Meri shook her head and cursed the tears that sprang to her eyes. "Do you even know why I did all those pageants?"

"Because you enjoyed them, of course." Her mother put on the fake, sugary smile she used for museum visits and long church sermons. "It's such fun to get dressed up and—"

"Because I wanted to spend time with you, Momma." Meri met her mother's eyes, so similar to her own, yet they saw the world in radically different colors. "The only time you were with me, and not at some charity function or some event, was when I did pageants. I needed a mother, and if having her meant standing on a stage and posing with a smile on my face, I did it."

Anna Lee's perfectly painted coral lips parted, closed. "I…I thought you enjoyed them. I thought you were having fun."

"Sometimes, yes, I did. But then when I won Miss North Carolina and it was time for the Miss America pageant, I couldn't do it anymore. I couldn't pretend for one more day, just to get a crown that I didn't even want. There were so many girls who truly did love the pageants and had worked harder than me and who deserved it far more than I did." She shook her head. "So I left. I didn't want to be known as a former Miss America contestant. I wanted to be known as just Meri Prescott."

"You deserved that crown, Meredith Lee. You deserved it more than anyone. You've worked so hard, and you can have it all back. If you talk to Bert, he can—"

"You're impossible." Meri blew her hair out of her face. Why did she keep hoping for change? Her mother hadn't done it in almost thirty years—she wasn't going to start now. "I'm leaving."

"Meredith Lee, do not embarrass me by storming out of here." Her mother kept her voice low, the tone harsh. Meri half expected her to threaten her daughter with grounding. "These people are your friends."

"None of them were my friends, Momma. And if you ever looked beneath the surface of anything in your life, you'd realize they were never yours either."

Her mother gasped. "My daughter would never talk to me like that."

"How would you know? You don't know your daughter any better than you know the guy who cleans the pool." Meri turned on her heel and walked away. Behind her, she could hear her mother sputtering, then switching gears to her polite voice as a guest came up to greet Anna Lee. Yet another sign that nothing had changed. Her mother was going to continue perpetuating this world made out of phony smiles.

Meri walked faster, hoping to get out of there before her mother could catch up or any of Anna Lee's guests could come up and talk to her. But she didn't move fast enough.

"Meredith Lee Prescott? Oh my goodness, you have changed!" Aspen Whitehall strode across the lawn— another grass-in-heels master—and gave Meri a small, practiced smile that showed just the right amount of perfectly straight and whitened teeth. Her blond hair was swept into a low chignon cemented in place by a whole lot of hair spray. Her brown eyes were turned blue by colored contacts—a secret only those who had competed with Aspen knew—and her slender body was emphasized with a little silicone on top and a little lipo on the bottom.

She had been Meri's replacement—the runner-up who went to the Miss America pageant when Meri bailed at the last minute. And as Meri looked at the fake, glossified woman before her, she realized this was what she would have become if she had stayed in Stone Gap.

"Aspen, I'm leaving. Have fun at the party."

"Wait." Aspen put a hand on Meri's arm. "Don't go yet. I wanted to talk to you."

"If this is about that pageant thing my mother wants me to do—"

"No. I, uh, wanted to ask you about that." Aspen pointed to the scar on Meri's cheek, then fluttered her hand down and gave Meri an embarrassed smile. "How... how do you live with that? I mean, all those years of worrying about how you look and now when you look in the mirror...I'm not trying to be mean, I'm just trying to understand how you learned to be..."

"Out in public with this hideous thing on my face?" Meri spat out the words, angry at her mother, angry at the guest list, angry at everything. "Sorry."

"Oh, goodness, no, don't apologize. That came out wrong. I don't think you look hideous. Not at all." Aspen shook her head and bit her lip. Moments passed, and as much as Meri wanted to leave, she sensed Aspen really wanted to talk. "How do you...well, how do you get to where you don't give a crap what people think of how you look?"

Meri let out a sharp laugh. "Is that what you think? I don't care?"

"God, no, this is coming out all wrong." Aspen fidgeted, her cheeks red. Once, the two girls had been friends—or as good of friends as one could get during a competition—and had even been roommates a time or two at pageants. They'd shared beauty tips and stage-fright episodes, caught in that world unto itself. For a moment, it seemed like they were sharing secrets over a despised vegetable tray in their room. "It's just…I saw you walk in here, and everyone was staring and you… you didn't care. You just did your job, and told off your mother, from what I heard, and I just think that's…cool."

"Cool? Me? You're the one who competed in Miss America."

"Only because you were strong enough to walk away. Don't get me wrong, I wanted to be Miss America. But I didn't win. And the day after the crowning, I realized that I had no life outside of pageants." She raised one shoulder, let it drop. "It was what we always talked about before—what would come next? And here I was at that next place, except I had no job, no career, no experience in my life except at being pretty and perfect and cutting ribbons at events."

"You're a great writer, Aspen. You should do that." Meri remembered the stories that Aspen had shared with her when they roomed together. Aspen had spent her nights scribbling in a thick journal, writing novels that she never published.

She shrugged. "Who's gonna take me seriously?"

"It doesn't matter. It only matters if one person does."

"Who's that?"

"You." She had echoed Jack's words and realized now how true they were. It didn't matter what anyone in this town or in her life or in New York thought of Meri. It only mattered what she thought. She reached out and drew Aspen into a quick hug. "I gotta go. I have a long-overdue date to get to."

There was nothing left on Jack's to-do list, and the day stretched before him, long and empty and hot. The garage was closed for the day, without a single car in the bay to be fixed. The few renovation projects he had on his own list were waiting on a shipment from the home improvement store. Jack had gone for a run, gone for a swim, wandered around at loose ends for another hour, then gone over to visit with Ray, but had found Meri's grandfather napping in his chair and decided to leave the old man alone. Luke had called twice to see if Jack had changed his mind about the Prescott party.

Jack hadn't. He hadn't, in fact, decided what to do after last night. It had been a wonderful, amazing, in-credible night, and in the warm and cozy glow after sex, he'd made plans for a future with Meri.

Then he'd gone to bed and realized what he had done. He couldn't plan a future with Meri. Couldn't date her. He was the last man in Stone Gap, hell, on planet Earth, who should be falling in love with Eli Delacorte's cousin.

Damn it. He'd screwed up again. Why couldn't he just leave Meri alone?

Jack headed away from Ray's, and turned down the wooded path that led back to his cottage. He ducked under a low branch, telling himself it would be good to sit on the porch, have a beer, maybe two, and just wait for this day to end and another to start. Maybe then he could find something to fill the hours of tomorrow and the day after that. The days that he knew would never be filled the way these last two weeks had been. Because

Meri was going to leave—and he needed to reconcile himself to that.

He passed a wide oak tree and his steps stuttered. Every time he took this path, he turned right at the fork instead of left, going toward his cottage instead of toward this place. Every time, except this time. Coincidence? Or some buried masochistic need to keep revisiting the past?

Jack put a hand on the tree, its base as wide as the trunk of a car, and the memories slammed into him, hard and fast. He was ten years old again, Eli only nine, and they were on an adventure, a quest they'd called it, to build a fort.

Come on, Jack, hurry up! We gotta get this finished before the storm hits.

Jack, running after Eli, his father's too-big tool belt banging hard against his hip and the planks of wood under his arm making his steps lurch to the right. The boys had dropped their wood into a pile, then shimmied up the tree—like two monkeys in the wild, Ray always called them. For an hour, Eli and Jack had hammered and sawed, fashioning a platform in the graceful arch between two large branches. They'd nailed the few remaining stubs of wood into the bark of the oak tree and added a thick knotted rope for a handhold to help them climb up to their new supersecret hideaway.

When they were done, they'd stayed up in the tree while the rain pattered the platform below them and the leaves above caught the worst of the storm. Every day that summer, he and Eli had come to the tree and climbed up to their fort, adding a tarp the following week, a battered pair of lawn chairs the week after that and a box filled with cans of soda and Twinkies.

Jack spread his palm across the rough bark of the

oak tree, fingers reaching for the first wooden slat, worn down now from years of storms and squirrels. He closed his eyes and leaned his head against the tree.

This is the best fort ever, Eli had said. *I hope it never falls down.*

Eli had gotten his wish, Jack thought. His throat caught, his heart ached, and his fingers gripped the slat, gripped it hard, then, before he could stop himself, he was tearing at it, tugging the wood until the nails gave way and the piece yielded with a protesting creak. Jack flung it at the ground, but seeing the broken piece on the bed of pine needles at his feet only made his heart break.

"Jack?"

Meri's voice, coming at him both like a balm and a flaming arrow. God, why couldn't she just walk away? Just forget about him once and for all?

"Leave me alone, Meri. Just leave me alone." He waited, his head against the tree, for the crunch of leaves beneath her feet.

"I'm not going anywhere, Jack. I left the party and came here. To see you."

He closed his eyes and fought the ache in his gut. How he wanted to have her in his arms, to have her in his life. But then he rounded back to square one again, the place where he was the one who let her cousin die, and he couldn't find a way to fashion some fairy-tale ending. "I don't think that's a good idea, Meri. I think we should just…end it here."

Silence. Long, cold silence. "End it here?"

"You're going back to New York, and dating or anything like that would just be impossible. I'm not a commitment kind of guy, and I'd hate to lead you on and make you think this meant something." The words ripped at his throat, but far better for her to think he was an ass than to know the truth. "I'm sorry."

Jack told himself it was best this way, like ripping off a Band-Aid. Yeah, if that was so, then why did it feel more like he had severed a limb?

There was no crunch of leaves. No receding footsteps. He spun around to see her still there.

"I told you, I'm not going anywhere."

"Why? Why are you still here? Why are you even still in Stone Gap? Your grandfather is doing better, you're back to taking pictures, why haven't you gone back to New York?"

"Because I haven't finished healing yet," she said softly. She came up beside him, and put a hand on his shoulder. "And neither have you."

He shrugged off her touch. "I'm fine."

"You are far from fine. I hear it in your voice when you lash out at me. I see it in the way you try not to connect with anyone. Your family, my grandfather, me. Yet at the same time, I see this longing in your face, for the people you love. You are building walls as fast as you can, while a part of you is still trying to tear them down. Like last night, those walls came down, but now they're back with a vengeance."

Damned if she didn't analyze him with the precision of a sniper. "Why are you here?"

"Honestly? Because I haven't given up hope on you yet." She reached out, as if she was going to touch him, then lowered her hand at the last second. "We both have scars, Jack. The only difference is, people can see mine. Yours are deep inside and if you don't tend to them, they will harden and spread until you can't find the man you used to be anymore."

"He's been gone for a long time, Meri."

"I think he's still there." She ran a hand through her hair, resettling the blond waves along her shoulders. "I've seen him dozens of times over the last couple of weeks. In the way you take care of my grandpa, the way you watch out for your father, and…in the way you look at me."

He tore his gaze away. "You're wrong."

"I think you're scared, Jack. Terrified of letting people know you aren't perfect. That you screw up and you fail, just like the rest of us." She took a step closer and slid her hand into his. "Failure is liberating, Jack. Admitting you aren't perfect sets you free."

He scoffed. "It's not as easy as that."

"It is." Her green eyes met his, true and earnest, and full of a belief he didn't feel. "You just have to let go and trust that the people who love you will catch you when you fall."

Chapter Fourteen

People who loved him? People like…Meri?

Jack did not dare to ask, because if she said yes, then he would have to do something about that information. Something like admit how he felt about her. Something like build a relationship with her.

A relationship that would be built on lies and secrets.

Meri stepped over to the tree, looked up at the wooden boards nestled between the branches, then back at Jack. "This is the fort you built with Eli."

Jack nodded. He didn't trust his voice.

"I remember when you guys built that. And you wouldn't let me up there because I was a girl. So I ran ahead of you and Eli and climbed up the rope—" she gave the knotted line a little swat and it swung back and forth "—then pulled it up with me so you two couldn't follow."

"And you ate every last one of our Twinkies."

She grinned. "That's what you got for telling me I couldn't go up there." Then she sighed and wrapped her arms around herself. "I miss Eli so much. Every time I turn around, I expect him to come walking into Grandpa Ray's, raiding the refrigerator and messing up my hair."

It was Jack's fault that Eli wasn't ever going to walk into Ray's kitchen again. It was Jack's fault that Eli would never climb this tree or sit in that fort again. It was Jack's fault that Meri was missing him, and always would.

Jack tore away from the tree, stumbling over the slat of wood on the ground. "I have to go."

"Wait. Don't go yet. I need your help."

The last word paused his step. "Help? I can't help you, Meri." *I can barely help myself.*

"You just have to stand there. That's all I need."

He pivoted back to her. "Stand here?"

"And let me take your picture."

"What? Why?"

"Because…" She fiddled with the camera around her neck. "I don't have any pictures of you. Not a single one. And no matter what happens, I want to remember you, just like this, in these woods where we all grew up."

He never should have gotten close to Meri again. Never should have slept with her. Even when he tried to drive her away, she stayed in his life, the only thing sweet and good—and the one thing he didn't deserve.

"I'm not really…"

"Just stay right there." She put up a palm. "Give me a second. Please, Jack?"

He shifted his weight. He should leave, go home. But his feet refused to move. "Okay."

She squinted through the eyepiece, adjusted the lens, then snapped a photo. Another. Turned the camera ninety degrees, took another. Stepped back, refocused, then took a fourth, a fifth. "Great shot," she said. "Lean against the tree, would you?"

He did as she asked, because he couldn't seem to find the strength to walk away, to end it once and for all. He watched her work, her face a mask of concentration, her pale pink dress puddling on the ground when she crouched. She asked him to bend down, rest one elbow on his knee, and prop his chin on his hand. Although he felt like someone pretending to be modeling for a JCPenney catalog, he did as she asked.

Meri's smile bloomed wider and wider on her face with each image. She was enjoying this, finding her rhythm. And he was enjoying watching her, as much as he knew he should let her go.

After a while, Meri lowered the camera. "Okay, I'm done torturing you."

He got to his feet and brushed the leaves off his shorts and legs. "It wasn't torture."

"I've been on the other side of that lens. I know how torturous it can be." She cocked her head and studied him. "You know, you should try it."

"Try what?" Try leaving, that's what he should do, but once again, his feet refused to bow to common sense.

"Seeing how the world looks through a lens. It changes things somehow."

He shook his head. "Nothing's going to change my view."

She lifted the camera off her neck and held it out to him. "You won't know unless you try."

He backed up, warding her off. "Meri—"

"You said all you see when you look out there is death and danger and hell." She lifted the Nikon in his direction. The glassy lens caught the sun and winked at him. "Maybe if you change the way you're looking at the world, Jack, the images you see will change, too."

The oak tree's shade spread over them in a wide, dark circle. A breeze fluttered through the woods and caught on the edge of the tattered tarp, flapping it in the wind. Was that a message from Eli? If so, Jack couldn't read it.

"I should leave," Jack said. Maybe if he said it enough times his feet would finally obey his brain.

"Just try, Jack." She moved the Nikon closer. "Once. That's all I ask."

He hesitated, then realized she wasn't going to give up, so he took the camera from her and peeked through the viewfinder. "All I see is a lot of green."

"You need to focus." She slid into place behind his right shoulder, reaching past him to guide the zoom back, widening the image before him. That cherry-almond perfume wafted up to tease him, lure him closer. "There. Try again."

He sighed and looked through the viewfinder a second time. The oak tree's bark filled the screen and Jack's vision blurred.

"Tell me, what do you see?"

"A tree," he barked. Why was he doing this? It was pointless. Wasn't going to change a damned thing. Yet even as he resisted, a part of him—the part that was still searching for peace and still believed in the impossible—held on, wanting Meri to be right.

A gentle hand on his arm, her voice soft against his ear. "Look some more."

He let out a breath and did what Meri asked. He shifted to the right, then concentrated on what he saw through the glass of the lens.

A spindly sapling, struggling for light and real estate among the thicker, ancient oaks that dominated this stretch of woods. A few ferns, content to live in the shadows at the base of the trees, spreading their leafy dark green fronds like aunts offering hugs. A squirrel darting among the ferns in a flash of brown fur and a flick of a bushy tail.

"What do you see?" Meri asked softly.

A white butterfly fluttered in the undergrowth, then flitted out of his line of sight. A shadowy pile of leaves against a fallen log covered a shadowed entrance for a rabbit or a squirrel. Dark green leaves hugged the head of a flower, about to bud any day, its lilac petals straining against the protective confines.

"Beauty," he whispered. "I see…beauty."

"That's what I see, too, Jack. True beauty, not the manufactured kind." She was crouched beside him, her presence a calming blanket. "Take a picture."

"How do I…"

She put a finger on top of the camera. "Press that button."

"But if it comes out all blurry or something, won't that mess you up?"

She laughed. "Photography is an art, and art is messy. It doesn't matter if it's blurry or if you take five hundred pictures of the same leaf. The important thing is that you have fun with it."

It took him several shots—okay, maybe two dozen—before the organized, regimented side of Jack let go and he began to snap a picture of whatever took his fancy. He turned the camera this way and that, zoomed in and out, aimed high, aimed low. When he tired of the landscape, he turned toward Meri and took a picture of her.

She giggled. "What are you doing?"

"Photographing a beautiful woman." He gestured toward her. "Stay there. The light is perfect. It makes your whole face glow."

She swung her hair over her cheek, covering the scar. "Okay."

He stepped forward and brushed the hair back behind her ear, just as he had that day in the grocery store. "You are beautiful the way you are, Meri."

"This isn't beautiful, Jack. It's a scar."

"Don't you understand, Meri? Scars show you have survived a battle." He trailed his finger along the mark that had changed Meri, made her better, stronger. "In the military, they're like a badge of honor because scars say you weren't afraid to dive into the fray and stand up for those you cared about, and for what was right."

"I didn't dive into a fray or fight a battle. I was attacked. Simply for being on the wrong street at the wrong time."

"You fought back, though, didn't you? And you survived. And you drove into this town among these people who thought you were nothing more than a grown-up Barbie doll, and you didn't cover up or look away or hide. You were proud and strong and pretty damned amazing."

She shook her head. "I haven't been strong. I have been kind of hiding here at Grandpa's. Trying to get my crap together so that I can go back to the life I had. Or find the next life I want."

"And what is in that life you want?"

A soft smile stole over her face, the kind that said she had dreams, hopes, wishes—all the things that Jack had left behind on that battlefield. In that moment, he was jealous as hell of Meri.

"I want to live in a place where I am surrounded by beauty so exquisite that all I want to do is take pictures all day. A place where there are people who love each other, and people I love. A place where…I fit in."

"Sounds a lot like Stone Gap to me."

She let out a chuff. "I've never fit in here. I never became what my mother expected, what this town expected…"

"You're even better than I expected."

She grinned. "You're just buttering me up. Probably for another dare."

"Not at all." He paused for a second, then put up a finger. "But I do reserve the right to use that toward another naked dare in the very near future."

God, he couldn't stop himself. Thirty minutes ago he'd been breaking up with her, ending their relationship forever. And now he was thinking about taking her skinny-dipping again, talking about a future. A future he had no right to offer but that didn't stop him from craving it, needing it. Needing her.

"Okay, that's it." She giggled again. "The picture taking has warped your brain. Give it back to the professional."

He laid the camera in her outstretched palm, but didn't let go right away. "My brain might be warped, but I know you. You have changed, for the better, and this town would be lucky to have you living here, putting up pictures that remind people to see the world can be a beautiful place."

It could also be an ugly place, a horrible, terrible ugly place, but he refused to let that little dose of reality tarnish this moment in the woods with the sun kissing Meri's features.

"Why, Jack Barlow. You sound almost romantic."

"You must have me confused with my charmer brother, Luke."

"I've never confused you with your brothers. Or any other man." Her eyes met his for one long, hot second, then she looked away. "Let me just grab a couple more shots, then I'll let you go wherever you were going."

If he'd been a philosophical man, Jack would have said he was going nowhere fast. Instead he stepped to the side while Meri raised the camera again. Because he didn't want the moment to end, didn't want to emerge from these woods and go back to reality.

"Jack, don't move." Her voice was a hushed, urgent whisper. She focused the camera and took a couple shots.

He glanced to the side, then at the ground. "Is there a snake or something?"

"No. An indigo bunting. He's just beside your shoulder. Don't move. Let me take one more shot. This is awesome. I hardly ever see one of these birds."

Jack chanced a glance to his right. The squat bird stared back at him, black-tipped wings tucked tight against its body, the tuft of bright blue feathers on his head seeming almost neon in the light. The blue color extended onto its beak, giving it a silvery tint. The bunting cocked his head to one side, dark beady eyes watching Jack intently.

"What are the chances?" Meri whispered. "Do you remember how much Eli loved those birds?"

Hell, yes, he remembered. In their downtime one night in Afghanistan, Eli had drawn a picture of an indigo bunting on the back of an envelope. It had looked so realistic, Jack had half expected it to fly off the page. He could still see Eli's hands making quick magic with a pencil and a recycled piece of paper.

Afterward, Eli had tucked the drawing away in his pocket with a little embarrassed grin. *Makes me think of home, you know?* he'd said.

Yeah, Jack knew. And when Eli had died, Jack had taken that picture out of Eli's pocket and put it in an envelope, letting it wing its way all the way back from Afghanistan to Eli's mother in Stone Gap. He'd thought about writing a letter or something, but there were no words to explain what had happened, no way to make it better. No way to say, *I'm sorry Eli couldn't bring this home himself.* And now that drawing was tacked to the wall in Betty's bakery, beside a single gold star for the child she had lost. Because of Jack.

"One more picture, Jack," Meri said.

He glanced at the bird again. It took two little hops forward, still watching him, turning its head left, right, then left again. Jack raised his gaze and there was the fort, forgotten and tattered now, just a skeleton of what it had once been. It was as if he was watching Eli die all over again, sitting on that hard, dusty ground, screaming in helpless fury for a rescue that was already too late. The bird hopped closer still, until the thin branch began to yield to the bunting's weight. The bunting leaned toward Jack, its dark eyes inquiring, curious.

"Get out of here!" He shooed at the bird and it started with a squawk, then flew off. An instant later, it was gone.

"Why did you do that?" Meri let out a gust. "I had this great shot lined up. I was just waiting for the bird to turn a bit and—"

"Because he's dead, goddamn it." Jack cursed again

and turned away, stalking off into the woods. Heading anywhere but where that damned bird had gone.

Meri hurried up behind him. "The bird wasn't dead, Jack. He was—"

"Eli. Eli is the one who is dead. And I don't need some hearts-and-flowers reminder of what he used to love or what he's missing. What I need is to be left alone."

"Talk to me, Jack." Meri circled around him and blocked his path. "I miss Eli, too. Maybe if we talk about how hard it's been to lose him, maybe then we can, I don't know—" she paused, her eyes filling with tears "—help each other get through it. Because it feels like we're a triangle that is missing a corner and not talking about it makes it worse. It's like we're pretending he never existed. Eli is still here, Jack." She waved at the woods. "He's in that fort, he's in that bird, he's in these woods. You can't keep putting the memory of him behind those walls, because you aren't the only one who is hurting here."

The pain in Meri's face was like a hot poker stabbing Jack in the heart. He had caused that, and God, he would do anything to take it back, to do that day over again. "I can't talk about this." He stalked off again.

"What are you going to do?" She called after him. "Run away for the rest of your life?"

He kept going. "If that's what it takes. Yeah."

"And what, become a hermit, living in the woods and burying yourself in work because you keep blaming yourself for his death?"

Jack's steps slowed. Stopped. The woods seemed to go silent and heavy, Mother Nature holding one long, expectant, judgmental breath.

"I know, Jack," she said as she moved forward and

closed the distance between them. He didn't turn around, didn't face her. "Not everything, but I know you were there that day."

He swallowed hard, the bile in his throat burning all the way down to his stomach. "How…" The words jammed and he struggled to loosen them again. "How do you know?"

"I saw it in your eyes." She came up beside him and raised the camera, shifting it so the digital screen faced him. An image of himself popped up, zeroed in on just his eyes. Even he could see the dark shadows lingering there, the darkness. His smile was held hostage in the tight curve of his mouth.

"I've taken a lot of pictures since I learned how to use a camera," she said. "And I know pain when I see it. Yours goes bone deep, and when I thought about how Eli served with you, but you wouldn't talk about him, and how my grandfather said you had been through a lot over there, it began to make sense."

"None of it makes sense, Meri, don't you get that? He never should have died." Jack cursed and kicked at a log on the ground, sending it spiraling off into the woods. He kicked another, but it was too big and sent a searing pain through his foot. He let out a scream that came from some primal place deep inside him, a place he had buried for months, then he leaned down and picked up the log and chucked it hard and far into the woods. It landed with a crack against another tree, but still that didn't ease the pain. He pitched another log into the woods, another, then, when he ran out of logs, he threw leaves, sticks, anything within reach.

He was a dervish, throwing things without even seeing them, just wanting these feelings out, out, out. "He never should have died!" Jack yelled at the logs, the bird, the woods, the universe. "Never. Should. Have. Died. It should have been me, goddamn it. It should have been me who died that day!"

Meri watched him tear up the space around them, then, when his breath was coming in heaves and his hands finally stilled, she went to him and put a gentle hand on his shoulder. "It wasn't your fault, Jack."

"Yes, it was! I killed him, Meri." He jabbed a finger at his chest. "*I* did it. Not that goddamned IED."

"But you didn't plant that bomb, right? And you didn't set it off."

"That doesn't matter. I should have seen it. I should have seen the depression in the dirt. Should have known they would bury one there, at the crossroads, where it could hit anyone going any direction. It was my job, Meri. I was the NCO, the one in charge of that convoy. My job was to protect Eli, to protect all those soldiers in those trucks. To think ahead, to expect the worst, and most of all, to keep my soldiers safe. Don't you understand? I was their *leader*. And I led them straight into a trap." He cursed again, wishing there was a boulder to throw, hell, a skyscraper, anything that would release this pressure, that searing, painful pressure, like a valve he couldn't open. "Cochran lost an arm, and Higgins, God, he lost both legs. Madden may never see again, though she pretends she's gonna be just fine. And Eli—"

The word choked in his throat, lodged there like a brick. Jack ran a hand through his hair and let out a breath. The truth bulged inside him, an ugly beast too long confined. "Eli…took the brunt of the explosion. It tore through that truck like it was made of paper. One minute he was sitting next to me, cracking a joke, the next…" Jack shook his head. "I pulled him out of the truck, and I tried to stop the bleeding, to save him. But there was too much damage, too much blood. I tried, Meri, I tried, God knows I tried." Jack lowered to his knees, crumpling just as he had that day with Eli in his arms, but this time his arms were empty, his best friend's body cold and buried deep in the earth. "I tried so goddamned hard to save him."

And then she was there, her arm around him, her head on top of his and that cherry-almond scent coming at him like a rainbow after a summer storm. "I know you did. I know you did, Jack," she whispered. "You loved him as much as I did. Why would I ever think that you wouldn't try to save him? That you wouldn't have given your life for his? You did nothing wrong. Eli wouldn't blame you for what happened." She raised his chin until he was looking at her. "And neither do I."

In that moment, that unexpected moment of forgiveness and empathy, the wall in Jack's heart crumbled. The tears he had held back for over a year surged to the surface. A wave of grief washed over him, a tidal wave that racked his body, tore through his throat, exhaled with Eli's name.

Meri held him tight while the woods held their peace, silent sentries watching two people grieving a life gone too soon. Above them, the torn end of the fort's tarp flapped in the breeze. Maybe, yes, the bird and the fort had been a message, that Eli was still here, still in these woods. Still part of their lives.

When Jack was spent, he got to his feet. Meri gripped his hand. He gave hers a squeeze back, and she lifted a smile to him. Then she let out a gasp and pointed behind him. "Look, Jack. The bird is back."

The indigo bunting bloomed bright among the green trees around him. His head turned one way, another, then he seemed to dip his beak in their direction before lifting off and disappearing into the woods. "It's a sign," Jack said. He raised Meri's hands to his lips and gave them a kiss. "A sign that I'm not ready to move forward. Not until I take one more step."

Then he released her hands and headed back into the woods.

Chapter Fifteen

The next morning, Meri found her grandfather in the kitchen, standing at the stove, scrambling eggs. After the moment in the woods with Jack yesterday, she'd watched him go and returned to her cottage. She'd looked around at the small space and realized she couldn't hide here anymore. She needed to move forward, and if that meant moving on without Jack, so be it. She just had to wrap up a few things here and then she could go.

"Grandpa Ray, what are you doing?"

"Fixing breakfast."

She took the spatula from him and waved him toward a seat at the table. "Aren't you supposed to be taking it easy? What did the doctor say?"

"That I was fit as a fiddle. Well, as fit as a fiddle that's been playing 'The Devil Went Down to Georgia' one too many times, but still, good to go about my business."

"Wait. What?" She crossed her arms over her chest. "I thought you were sick. When I talked to you a few weeks ago, you said you were ordered to rest, take it easy, and that you needed help. You told me you were dying."

"An exaggeration. I was sick, but not dying. Yet." He shrugged. "I lied."

"Lied? But, Grandpa—"

"I wanted to see you. And you needed to be here. Last few times I talked to you, you sounded lost, Merry Girl, and you needed to come home to find yourself."

Her grandfather knew her well. If he hadn't called, she would have stayed in New York, aimlessly trying to get past the mugging, leaving the wounds of her past un-healed. She glanced out the window at the lake she loved so much, a lake that had brought her home, in more ways than one. "You're right. Kind of ironic that the first pic-ture I took after the attack was of this lake."

"Not ironic at all. It's fate." He took the spatula back and flipped the eggs. "You're meant to be here."

"Oh, I don't know about that. I don't fit here." The toaster popped, so Meri buttered two slices of wheat and laid them on a plate. "I'm that runaway beauty queen with the scar on her face. People are never going to see me as anything else."

"They will if you do."

Was it really that simple? She changed her perspec-tive and in the process, changed what others thought? She thought of the label on her camera. *Photography by Meri Prescott.* The day she'd affixed that to the camera's body had been a day like any other. It was the act of stamping herself a professional that changed how she felt inside.

"You may be right, Grandpa."

"I'm always right. It comes with age." He took a seat

at the table and dove into his breakfast. "Now, what about Jack?"

"What about Jack?" Meri poured a cup of coffee and leaned against the counter. It was the same question she'd been asking herself since yesterday. *What about Jack?*

"Have you married him yet?"

She spat out her coffee. "Married him? Where did you get that idea?"

"You have been in love with that boy your entire life, and don't you deny it." Grandpa Ray wagged a fork at her. "He's been in love with you, too. It's about time the two of you said it out loud and made it legal."

"We're just getting to know each other again. We've been apart a long time and…" Her gaze narrowed. "Wait. Have you been trying to push us together? The fishing trip you were too tired to go on? The dinner at the Barlows that you skipped? All those times you were napping and we were left alone?"

"Like I said, you don't get to be my age without getting a few extra brain cells in your noggin." He tapped at the white hair on his head.

She leaned over and pressed a kiss to her grandfather's cheek. "You are a hopeless romantic."

He waved off her words. "Don't let that get around town. Before you know it, I'll have every single woman over the age of sixty trying to be my girlfriend."

"I think you deserve that. And you need a woman to keep you in line, you matchmaking faker."

"Ah, I really was sick, but I really didn't need you to do all that you did." He reached out and grabbed her hand. "And I was selfish because I missed having you around."

"I've missed being here." She squeezed his hand. "You're totally forgiven for lying."

"Exaggerating." Through the open window, they heard the crunch of tires on the driveway. "Speaking of people you should forgive...I think that's the sound of your mother's car out there."

Meri rolled her eyes, then got to her feet and dumped out her coffee. "If she's here to yell at me again for messing up her perfect party, just tell her I left."

"Sorry, but it's time for my nap." Grandpa got to his feet, then turned back at the doorway. "Besides, it'll do you good to talk to her. She's a difficult woman, your mother, but she loves you."

Meri scoffed, but headed outside anyway. Her mother was just stepping out of the Cadillac, wearing a butter-yellow pantsuit and cream-colored heels. Her hair was swept into a bun and she had on oversized sunglasses.

"I wanted to talk to you." Her mother's tone was clipped and tight.

Oh, joy. Meri crossed her arms over her chest. "Then let's talk."

"Not here in the middle of the driveway." Anna Lee's nose wrinkled. "Somewhere...quiet."

"It's too beautiful to stay indoors," Meri said. "Let's go down to the lake."

Anna Lee readied a protest, then bit it back and gestured to Meri to lead the way. In her flip-flops, Meri easily navigated the path, but her mother had to take her time, picking her way across the roots and divots in the earth. An ironic twist to the garden party, when Anna Lee had been at home in her heels and Meri had been the one out of place. Maybe for once her mother understood what it felt like to be the one out of place. Instead of rubbing it in, Meri reached out a hand and helped Anna Lee over the last bit of rough terrain.

"Thank you," Anna Lee said. She cast a dubious look at the wooden bench facing the lake, but settled on the seat beside her daughter. "I wanted to talk about the party," her mother began.

"If this is another complaint about how I behaved and what I—"

"It's not." Anna Lee put up a hand. "I want to apologize."

Meri stared at her mother, sure she was hearing things. "Apologize?"

"For pushing you into those pageants. I should have listened to what you wanted instead of making you do them. I never realized how much you hated it."

"I didn't *always* hate it, Momma. There were times when it was fun to get all dressed up and to walk down a runway with a spray of roses and a shiny crown on my head. I just didn't like it becoming my whole life. What I ate, what I wore, what I did in my free time. Everything was about how it would impact a pageant."

"I'm sorry. I thought I was giving you a future."

"How would pageants give me a future?"

Anna Lee laid her hands in her lap and lowered her gaze to her French manicure. "I was never an especially smart or talented girl. I didn't excel at anything, really, except being pretty. I grew up poorer than a mouse in a basket, and my mama always told me that I had to do whatever it took to preserve my looks because they were going to be my future. The only way I could support myself."

"By marrying well."

"And I did. I told myself I was happy." Anna Lee's voice held the poignant note of might-have-beens. "For a while, I was, I guess. But the thing about relying on your looks is that they eventually go away and then you're left with…nothing."

"You don't have nothing, Momma. You have done more charity work than anyone in Stone Gap. The money you raised helped build schools, start that community garden, renovate the animal shelter. You've left a legacy, Momma. That's something and not something everyone does." Meri reached out and covered her mother's hand with her own. "I'm proud of you."

Anna Lee scoffed. "You're proud of me? I've always been the one proud of you, though I didn't tell you nearly enough. I was proud when you won all those pageants, when you won Miss North Carolina, when you were bound for Miss America. But I have to say—" she let out a breath "—I was proudest of you the day you walked away from all that, and prouder still when you came back here, after what happened to you. You're a braver girl than me, Meri, and I'm sorry if I have ever implied you were anything less than perfect."

Tears choked Meri's voice. "Thank you, Momma."

She gave Meri's fingers a squeeze. "None of those things you say I did mean anything to me, not if I've lost you." Her lower lip trembled and her perfect smile slid. "Do I…do I still have you?"

Meri nodded. "You always will."

A tear slid down Anna Lee's face, marring her makeup, but she made no move to swipe it away. Instead she drew her daughter's hand into her lap, and the two of them sat there for a long time, hands clasped, watching life go by on the lake.

If Jack Barlow ever made a list of all the stupid things he had done in his life, he would surely run out of ink before he got to the end. At the top of the list was telling Meri Prescott that their relationship was over.

After the afternoon in the woods, he had gone home rather than go after her. It had been an agonizing night, but he'd needed the time to process, to think, to be sure.

When dawn broke, Jack realized that no matter how he felt about Meri, he couldn't go after her—couldn't be the man he needed to be—until he stopped running from his demons. So on a pretty Monday morning when he had a long list of things to do, he set that list aside, climbed in the truck and headed into town.

He parked outside the bakery and headed inside. It was early yet—the bakery had only opened five minutes earlier—and there was only one customer buying some bread for that night's dinner. Betty Delacorte greeted Jack with a big smile, then came over to him when the customer left. "Good morning, Jack! What can I get you to eat?"

"I'm not here to eat, Miz Delacorte." He shoved his hands into his pockets. "I'm here to talk to you and Mr. Delacorte. About…Eli."

The smile dimmed on her face. "I'll call him right now. And turn that sign to Closed."

"Oh, you don't have to do that. I don't want you to lose any business or anything."

"You want to talk about my Eli, don't you?"

He nodded.

"Then that is a reason to stop a moment and talk." She hustled next door to get George, and when they returned, she did as she'd said and turned the lock on the door.

The three of them sat at one of the small round tables at the front of the bakery. Jack let his gaze rest on the penciled drawing of the indigo bunting, then started to talk. He talked until his voice grew hoarse and until he'd told it all, from the day Eli first came to him to the day he had put the drawing in the mail. He glossed over the details of Eli's death, but otherwise left nothing out, finally, fully coming clean.

After he was done, Betty was the first to get to her feet and draw Jack into a hug. George told Jack he was glad they'd finally talked, then wrapped a beefy arm around both of them and the three of them sat there for a long time, grieving their loss.

"I'm so sorry," Jack said. "I should have come sooner. I should have told you all of it a year ago. Should have written a letter when I sent you that drawing. Should have done a hell of a lot of things that I didn't. I just…I couldn't bear to hurt you any more than I already had."

"You didn't hurt us," George said. "You gave us answers. And a connection to our boy. The stories you told, they were about him, about how he was brave and strong and everything we ever wanted." A watery smile filled his face, and George's blue eyes held Jack's for a long time. "Thank you."

Those were the last words Jack had ever expected to hear. They humbled him, and gave him that elusive gift he had been seeking for so long.

Peace.

And an idea.

Meri was loading up her car when Jack pulled into the driveway later that day. When she saw him swing out of his truck and lope over to her, her step faltered and she almost dropped the box in her arms. Damn, he was a good-looking man. She had loved him almost all her life, and knew in her heart she was never going to stop. Heck, loving Jack Barlow was part and parcel of what made up her DNA. That was what made seeing him today ten times more painful. She clutched the box tight to her chest and willed her face to stay impassive, calm.

"Where are you going?" he asked.

"Back to New York." She turned away and stowed the box in the trunk, beside her suitcase. Despite what her grandfather had said this morning, she already knew where this would end with Jack. He had broken up with her, after all, and driven her away twice now. She needed to leave, to get back to her life, before he hurt her a third time. "My grandpa is doing well now, and I need to decide if I'm going to take that job at the travel magazine or not."

"Don't go. Not yet. I want to show you something." He put out a hand. "Will you come with me?"

She hesitated. She was ready to leave, had cemented her decision to go, but seeing Jack again, her heart did that funny little flippity-flop and she knew that if he asked, she'd go to the moon and back with him. "Okay. But I really do have to get on the road soon."

Yeah, look how well her resolve was holding up so far. Why did he have to look so damned good?

"We won't be long. I promise." He helped her up into his truck, made sure she was buckled, then turned the pickup around and headed back to town. The truck bumped over the rutted lake road, jostling Meri into brushing up against Jack's arm. The connection sent a searing heat through her. Okay, so maybe forgetting him wasn't going to be as easy as she thought.

Meri held on to the handle on the passenger's side door and tried to cement herself in the seat. "Where are we going?"

"You'll see." A smile played on his lips as he drove away from the lake, past the mansions and down to the quaint downtown area, where it seemed as if time had stopped two hundred years in the past.

As much as Meri loved New York, she loved this, too. Loved the homey feeling of Stone Gap, the way the entire town felt like walking into a much-loved aunt's home. When she'd been younger, she'd seen Stone Gap as a prison, marching her down to a sentence she wanted to escape. But now, after leaving and returning, and most of all, coming into her own as an adult, she realized she loved this quirky little town.

Jack parked the truck in front of a small vacant lot to the west of Aunt Betty's bakery. He shut off the engine, then got out, coming around to open her door and help her down. The little act of chivalry melted her heart a little. Damn it. He was good-looking and nice to her.

Meri crossed her arms over her chest, stood on the sidewalk and looked at the empty dirt patch before her. Just get this over with, get on the road, as soon as possible. "Um…what is this?"

"Nothing right now. But it's going to be a playground. With a fort over there, and a tree right there. A set of swings, a slide, and some monkey bars on that side." He pointed and waved his hands, showing his vision for what was to come, the idea that had blossomed in his head that morning. He had some preliminary sketches sitting in his truck and had already started planning out the assembly and materials list. Maybe this could be the first step to that carpentry business Luke had told him to start. Jack liked the idea of building things where once there had been nothing. Liked that a lot. "And everything is going to be painted indigo bunting blue."

She turned to him, a smile curving across her face as the pieces fell into place and she realized what he was creating. "For Eli?"

Jack nodded. "Betty and George have owned this lot for years, thinking they'd expand or build a parking lot or something, but when I told them today that I wanted a way to honor Eli's memory, they thought there was no better place than here. I've been searching for a purpose, Meri, a way to…keep him alive, I guess. And what better way to do that than to preserve it, here, in this town he loved so much."

"I can't think of a better way to honor his memory, Jack. He would have loved it." She slipped her hand into his, such a simple gesture, but it warmed Jack from the inside out. "I love it."

"Good." He turned her to face him, to tell her the real reason he had brought her out here. When he'd seen her loading her car today, his heart had stopped. But she was here now, and he took that as a good sign. "Because I'm going to need help. Your help."

Confusion muddled her green eyes. "I can't hammer or cut wood or anything like that."

"That's what my brother Luke is for. I don't need you for your building skills, Meri." He took both her hands now, drawing her to him, so close he could see the flecks of gold in her eyes, catch the familiar scent of cherries and almonds. "I need you to help me make it beautiful. You have vision and an eye for that kind of thing. I'm the brawn, but you're the creativity."

She tugged her hands out of his and took a step back. "I'm going back to New York, Jack. Maybe we can talk out some ideas by email, but I won't be here to help you build this."

"So you're running away?"

She avoided his gaze. "I'm not running. I have a job offer in New York. A career."

"A career you could just as easily have here." Jack stepped into her space, his height casting a shadow over her. Still she wouldn't look at him, and he worried that he was too late. That he had waited too long and lost her before he ever really had her again. "What are you afraid of, Meri?"

"I'm not afraid of anything."

"Liar." He grinned, then cupped her face and waited for her gaze to connect with his. He saw fear flicker on her face, a fear he knew well. "I know you, better than I know myself sometimes. And I know exactly what you're afraid of, because I'm afraid of it, too."

"Jack—"

She tried to turn away but he didn't let her go. Couldn't let her go, not until he had said what he'd brought her here to say.

"Remember that day we caught crawdads in the creek? You didn't want to go down to the water and get your dress dirty, so I climbed down there, caught the biggest one I could find and brought it back to you." He took her hand and splayed her palm, as if they were ten and twelve again, standing in the summer sunshine while the water babbled a gentle song. "I dropped it in your hands, and I thought you'd scream but you didn't. Instead, you looked up at me with the biggest smile I've ever seen. I didn't know it then, but I know it now. That was the day I fell in love with you."

She scoffed. "Jack, we were kids. You couldn't possibly have been in love then."

"Maybe so, but I do know from that day forward, I

thought about you all the time." He traced her lip with his thumb and thought she had to be the most beautiful woman he had ever seen. Not just on the outside, but on the inside, too, in the way she tended to her grandfather, worried about him, saw the world around her. Meri had opened his eyes to the beauty that existed in his heart, in his world, and for that, he could never repay or thank her. All he could do was go on loving her. "Do you know why I waited so long to ask you out? Because we were friends first, and next to Eli, you were the best friend I ever had. I didn't want to screw that up. In the end, I did anyway, by breaking up with you. I was so mean that day in the garage, Meri. I was a jerk, and I'm sorry."

A sad smile filled her face. "No, you were a reality check. I didn't like what you had to say and I spent about a year being mad at you for saying it, but you were right. I was becoming the very thing I didn't want to be. Your words eventually gave me the courage to walk away from all that I knew and start over again in New York. Doing what I wanted to do, not what someone else prescribed for me."

He could only imagine how much strength that had taken, for her to give up her crown, turn down the penultimate pageant and start from scratch in a whole new city. "You are a beautiful, incredible, strong woman, Meredith Prescott," he said to her, looking deep into her eyes, past the scar that he no longer saw, "and I hope to God I haven't lost you a second time."

A heartbeat passed between them. Cars drove down the street, the soft *whoosh* of their tires along the pavement serving as a quiet undertow for the voices of people moving around the downtown area. But Meri didn't hear any of them. She only heard the words Jack had said. *That was the day I fell in love with you.*

All this time, she'd thought she'd been the only one in love. That she'd been a silly schoolgirl with an unrequited crush. When it turned out the two of them had just been scared teenagers who didn't know what they were giving up. And now, if she ran off to New York, she'd be that same scared girl who could risk her career but had yet to risk her heart. Did she really want to be living in the city again, alone and regretting what might have been?

"You didn't lose me, Jack. Not in here." She placed a palm on her heart, then on his.

"Then stay here, with me. And let's build this playground and build a future. Right here in Stone Gap." He laid his hand over hers and she felt the steady *thump-thump* of his heart beneath her palm. It was as reliable and sure as this man. "You were right about me. I have so many scars deep inside me, scars I never thought could heal. Then you came along and reminded me that there is goodness in this world, a life that I still want. A life I want with you, Meri, because I love you."

The words settled over her heart like a butterfly landing on a flower. She held them, savoring them, for a long time, then wrapped her arms around his neck. "I love you, too, Jack. I always have."

A smile winged across his face, broad and real and joyous. "Then how about you try on one more title for size?"

"What title is that?"

"Mrs. Jack Barlow. It doesn't come with a crown, or even a fancy ribbon, and I can't promise that there will always be roses, but there will be plenty of opportunities to wear high heels and smile."

She laughed. Only Jack would throw the high heels perk into the mix. "Are there any other former beauty queens in contention for this title?"

He pretended to think for a second. "Nope. It's a lock. Although—" he gave her a teasing grin "—there may be a bathing suit competition."

"I thought I already won the skinny-dipping one."

"Oh, yes, you did. Ten times over. Scratch the bathing suit competition. In fact, scratch the bathing suit altogether."

She laughed again. "Mrs. Jack Barlow sounds like the perfect title for me." She rose on her tiptoes and pressed a kiss to his lips. He opened his mouth against hers and cradled her head in his hands. This kiss was sweet and slow, like molasses running through her veins, and she thought it was definitely possible to melt into someone. When she pulled back, she saw him watching her with those blue eyes that had seen the world and come back here, to her. How she was going to love seeing those eyes every morning for the rest of her life. "We do have one more thing to settle, Jack."

"What's that?"

"Somebody owes me a picnic with desserts. But right now, I think all we need is the blanket. The desserts can come later." She leaned into him again and kissed him a second time, less leisurely, more demanding, the fire erupting between them so quickly she could barely mumble, "Much, much later."

* * * * *

Don't miss Luke Barlow's story,
the next installment in
New York Times *bestselling author Shirley Jump's*
new miniseries,
THE BARLOW BROTHERS

Coming soon from Harlequin Special Edition!

Available January 20, 2015

#2383 FORTUNE'S LITTLE HEARTBREAKER
The Fortunes of Texas: Cowboy Country • by Cindy Kirk
When British aristocrat Oliver Fortune Hayes gets custody of his young son, he's stunned. But little does he know that much more is in store! Oliver's world is rocked like a rodeo when beautiful cowgirl Shannon Singleton saddles up as his son's nanny. Can Fortune and the free spirit ride off into the sunset for a happily-ever-after?

#2384 HER BABY AND HER BEAU
The Camdens of Colorado • by Victoria Pade
Beau Camden and Kyla Gibson were hot and heavy years ago, but their passionate romance didn't end well. Now Kyla's back in town with a secret or two up her sleeve. Named guardian to her cousin's infant girl, she has motherhood on her mind and isn't interested in reuniting with her ex. But the Camden hunk isn't going to take no for an answer when it comes to a happy ending with his former love!

#2385 THE DADDY WISH
Those Engaging Garretts! • by Brenda Harlen
Playboy CEO Nathan Garrett has no interest in making any permanent acquisitions in the marital department. He's happy living the single life! That is, until he shares one night of passion with his sexy secretary, Allison Caldwell, while they're stranded during a snowstorm. Now Nate is thinking a merger with the single mom and her adorable son might just be the deal of a lifetime...

#2386 THE FIREMAN'S READY-MADE FAMILY
The St. Johns of Stonerock • by Jules Bennett
Plagued by a tragic past, small-town fire chief Drake St. John is surprised when sparks fly with Marly Haskins. The beautiful single mom has only one priority—her daughter, Willow, whom she wants to protect from her ex. But where there's smoke, there's flame, and Drake and Marly can't resist their own true love.

#2387 MARRY ME, MACKENZIE! • by Joanna Sims
When bachelor businessman Dylan Axel opened his door for Mackenzie Brand, he had no idea that he'd find a whole new life on the other side. It turns out that their long-ago romance created a beautiful daughter, Hope, who's now sick. Can Dylan, Mackenzie and Hope each get a second chance to have life, love and the pursuit of a happy family?

#2388 HIS SMALL-TOWN SWEETHEART • by Amanda Berry
Down on her luck, Nicole Baxter is back home in Tawnee Valley to lick her wounds. She doesn't expect to come face-to-face with childhood friend Sam Ward, who's grown up into a drop-dead gorgeous man! When Sam puts his entire future at risk, it's up to Nicole to show him everything he wants is right there with her.

REQUEST YOUR FREE BOOKS!
2 FREE NOVELS PLUS 2 FREE GIFTS!

♥ HARLEQUIN®

SPECIAL EDITION
Life, Love & Family

YES! Please send me 2 FREE Harlequin® Special Edition novels and my 2 FREE gifts (gifts are worth about $10). After receiving them, if I don't wish to receive any more books, I can return the shipping statement marked "cancel." If I don't cancel, I will receive 6 brand-new novels every month and be billed just $4.74 per book in the U.S. or $5.24 per book in Canada. That's a savings of at least 14% off the cover price! It's quite a bargain! Shipping and handling is just 50¢ per book in the U.S. and 75¢ per book in Canada.* I understand that accepting the 2 free books and gifts places me under no obligation to buy anything. I can always return a shipment and cancel at any time. Even if I never buy another book, the two free books and gifts are mine to keep forever.

235/335 HDN F45Y

Name	(PLEASE PRINT)

Address	Apt. #

City	State/Prov.	Zip/Postal Code

Signature (if under 18, a parent or guardian must sign)

Mail to the **Harlequin® Reader Service:**
IN U.S.A.: P.O. Box 1867, Buffalo, NY 14240-1867
IN CANADA: P.O. Box 609, Fort Erie, Ontario L2A 5X3

Want to try two free books from another line?
Call 1-800-873-8635 or visit www.ReaderService.com.

* Terms and prices subject to change without notice. Prices do not include applicable taxes. Sales tax applicable in N.Y. Canadian residents will be charged applicable taxes. Offer not valid in Quebec. This offer is limited to one order per household. Not valid for current subscribers to Harlequin Special Edition books. All orders subject to credit approval. Credit or debit balances in a customer's account(s) may be offset by any other outstanding balance owed by or to the customer. Please allow 4 to 6 weeks for delivery. Offer available while quantities last.

Your Privacy—The Harlequin® Reader Service is committed to protecting your privacy. Our Privacy Policy is available online at www.ReaderService.com or upon request from the Harlequin Reader Service.

We make a portion of our mailing list available to reputable third parties that offer products we believe may interest you. If you prefer that we not exchange your name with third parties, or if you wish to clarify or modify your communication preferences, please visit us at www.ReaderService.com/consumerschoice or write to us at Harlequin Reader Service Preference Service, P.O. Box 9062, Buffalo, NY 14269. Include your complete name and address.

Newly promoted Nathan Garrett is eager to prove he's no longer the company playboy. His assistant, single mom Allison Caldwell, has no interest in helping him with that goal, despite the fiery attraction between them. But as Nate grows closer to Alli's little boy, she wonders whether he might be a family man after all…

Read on for a sneak preview of THE DADDY WISH, by award-winning author Brenda Harlen, the next book in the miniseries THOSE ENGAGING GARRETTS!

***

Allison sipped her wine. Dammit—her pulse was racing and her knees were weak, and there was no way she could sit here beside Nate Garrett, sharing a drink and conversation, and not think about the fact that her tongue had tangled with his.

"I think I'm going to call it a night."

"You haven't finished your wine," he pointed out.

"I'm not much of a drinker."

"Stay," he said.

She lifted her brows. "I don't take orders from you outside the office, Mr. Garrett."

"Sorry—your insistence on calling me 'Mr. Garrett' made me forget that we weren't at the office," he told her. "Please, will you keep me company for a little while?"

"I'm sure there are any number of other women here who will happily keep you company when I'm gone."

"I don't want anyone else's company," he told her.

"Mr. Garrett—"

"Nate."

She sighed. "Why?"

"Because it's my name."

"I meant, why do you want my company?"

"Because I like you," he said simply.

"You don't even know me."

His gaze skimmed down to her mouth, lingered, and she knew he was thinking about the kiss they'd shared. The kiss she hadn't been able to stop thinking about.

"So give me a chance to get to know you," he suggested.

"You'll have that chance when you're in the VP of Finance's office."

She frowned as the bartender, her friend Chelsea, slid a plate of pita bread and spinach dip onto the bar in front of her. "I didn't order this."

"But you want it," Chelsea said, and the wink that followed suggested she was referring to more than the appetizer.

"Actually, I want my bill. It's getting late and…" But her friend had already turned away.

Allison was tempted to walk out and leave Chelsea to pick up the tab, but the small salad she'd made for her own dinner was a distant memory, and she had no willpower when it came to three-cheese spinach dip.

She blew out a breath and picked up a grilled pita triangle. "The service here sucks."

"I've always found that the company of a beautiful woman makes up for many deficiencies."

***

*Don't miss THE DADDY WISH by award-winning author
Brenda Harlen, the next book in her new miniseries,*
THOSE ENGAGING GARRETTS!
*Available February 2015, wherever
Harlequin® Special Edition books and ebooks are sold.*
www.Harlequin.com

HSEEXPO115R

HARLEQUIN®

A *Romance* FOR EVERY MOOD™

**Stay up-to-date on all your
romance-reading news with the
Harlequin Shopping Guide,
featuring bestselling authors, exciting new
miniseries, books to watch and more!**

The newest issue will be delivered right to you
with our compliments! There are 4 each year.

Signing up is easy.

EMAIL

ShoppingGuide@Harlequin.ca

WRITE TO US

HARLEQUIN BOOKS
Attention: Customer Service Department
P.O. Box 9057, Buffalo, NY 14269-9057

OR PHONE

1-800-873-8635 in the United States
1-888-343-9777 in Canada

Please allow 4-6 weeks for delivery of the first issue by mail.

JUST CAN'T GET ENOUGH
ROMANCE
Looking for more?

5912

Harlequin has everything from contemporary, passionate and heartwarming to suspenseful and inspirational stories.

**Whatever your mood,
we have a romance just for you!**

❤ HARLEQUIN®

A *Romance* FOR EVERY MOOD™

www.Harlequin.com

SERIESHALOAD